SHADE
THOSE LAURELS

SHADE
THOSE LAURELS

by
CYRIL CONNOLLY

concluded by
PETER LEVI

Pantheon Books   New York

Library of Congress Cataloging-in-Publication Data

Connolly, Cyril, 1903–1974.
Shade those laurels / by Cyril Connolly ; concluded by Peter Levi.
p.   cm.
I. Levi, Peter.   II. Title.
PR6005.0393S5 1991   823'.912—dc20   91-52620
ISBN 0-679-40433-3

for

DEIRDRE

SHADE
THOSE LAURELS

INTRODUCTION

This is a short novel left unfinished by Cyril Connolly; he wrote three parts out of four and published the first part in *Encounter* in March 1956. The second and third parts were typed but not finally corrected: there are small mechanical errors in them, such as personal names altered in *Encounter* but left wrong in the typescript. Since Cyril was a tireless self-critic, who achieved many of his best results in correcting his typescripts and many proofs, this is an important point. Not a line of the last part was ever written, though he did once get out the typescript or the notebook (I recollect a manuscript notebook) a few years before his death, with the idea of finishing the story. It was around that time that he showed me part two, and told me the secret of his plot. In this story, as in all his writings, he was both intimately personal and elusive. The place names and personal names are false trails; Kemble is one of his own family names, but that means little because, like every novelist, he is all his characters and yet stands apart from them all. Those readers who prefer to come upon the *dénouement* in its rightful place had better stop reading this introduction at once.

He told me that the clue to his mystery was the Gassendi Club, an invented Oxford undergraduate dining club of the 1920s, whose members had combined to play a deliberate trick on the public. One had become a publisher, one a critic, and so on, and they worked together in a secret combination to occupy the commanding heights of the literary world. Sir Mortimer wrote none of his books: they secretly wrote them in committee or, as fashion altered, they captured some penniless young writer to transform the style in whatever was the fashionable direction. Sir Mortimer only impersonated a great man, while all the old friends had sacrificed their own careers as writers to the same scheme, for the sake of financial advantage. Julian was the last of the fashionable ghost-writers, but at the fatal dinner party he was being sacked, while the new young man, Stephen Kemble, was being tested for the job. But alas, Sir Mortimer had decided that night to write a book of his own at last. The others could not allow him to do so, as he was too much of a fool or a phoney, or anyway because he wrote so badly.

I do not believe Cyril had worked out his solution in full detail. For example, I am not sure how much Cressida knew (everything perhaps), or quite how they intended to keep Julian quiet for the rest of his life. In the second and third parts I do detect a certain falling off, at least in its present state. The story as first conceived was a light-hearted *jeu d'esprit*, like *Bond Strikes Camp* and *Missing Diplomats*, and the *Sunday Times* version of *White Mischief*. It reminds me of something Edmund Wilson wrote in *Classics and Commercials* (p. 285, quoted by Michael Sheldon in *Friends of Promise*) about those ". . . who are born with a gift of style, a natural grace and wit, so that their jobs have the freshness of *jeux d'esprit* and sometimes their *jeux d'esprit* turn out to stick as classics". But I suspect he planned *Shade Those Laurels* at too great length, and therefore got tired of it. It exists almost entirely for the sake of its amazing dinner party. All the same, it is a pity it should get lost, yet in order to be printed it has to be finished: under modern conditions no publisher is interested in printing a mere two-thirds of a novel, even by Cyril. I have taken on the task of writing the final section in a spirit of pure professionalism: I have no illusion about my own prose style or about the subtle and brilliant qualities of Cyril's intellect and senses, or his wide and peculiar learning. My task is to tack a bit of calico on to the end of a wonderful fragment of tapestry earlier in taste and period. I am unashamed of doing that in order to preserve what there is of the tapestry.

I have always felt passionately about *Shade Those Laurels*. I read it on the train, going to France and Italy for the first time, in the early spring of 1956, identifying heavily with Mr Kemble. I was an Oxford undergraduate, having just finished classical mods. I had never been abroad before though I was already twenty-five. Switzerland awaited me, with mountains standing up around the lakes and the strange sensation of being greeted as an *Altphilologieprofessor*, and Venice, where you walk out of the station into a Guardi, and Florence, where I lived in the Villa Machiavelli and snow blew in through shut double windows, and the wolves ate a postman. That holiday after mods is usually wonderful, but it was more so for me, because I had left school at seventeen to become a Jesuit and a lot of the fizz in my temperament had therefore been bottled up for eight years. I lavished on Cyril as a writer those affections and loyalties that no doubt ought to have been devoted to duller authors and heavier matters.

I remember one afternoon that winter term discussing with my friend Denis Bethell what we would do if we were Pope, like Hadrian VII. "You," he said, "would begin by canonising Cyril Connolly." Later on, when I got to know this admirable writer, who by that time was like a Chinese sage, wreathed suddenly in similes, and who had given up smoking and, later, drink in order to preserve his senses and his consciousness intact for work, my adoration was transformed into a deeper kind of delight. I had joined the throng of those who could not avoid loving him, but there was something more, so that I still find it hard to avoid taking Dryden's words personally, even though there have been so many with more right:

> But you, whom ev'ry Muse and Grace adorn
> Whom I foresee to better fortune born
> Be kind to my remains; and, Oh, defend
> Against your judgement your departed friend!
> Let not th'insulting Foe my fame pursue
> But shade those laurels which descend to you.

PETER LEVI

April 1990
The Orangery
Frampton-on-Severn

4

PART I

Eyes, Look Your Last

As if divining my disappointment: "Read that last sentence again, Kemble," he interrupted.

"And more, perhaps, than any man living," I continued, *"Sir Mortimer appreciates and has taught others to appreciate the things which we can touch or see – this visible world."*

"Yes, it's good," went on my editor – "so much better than the one we're using. A thousand pities you're not a celebrity: it's names we like on this paper, especially when a famous author, whom most of our readers have never heard of – ha! – gets a knighthood on his birthday. Tell you what: I'll change a letter here and there and we can turn it into something. *'More perhaps than any man now living, Sir Mortimer appreciated the things which he could touch or see!'* I never liked to scrap a good bloke or a good sentence. Take care of this and we'll run you off a proof when you come back – meanwhile don't let him grab it. He mightn't think it funny."

"But really, I can't let you do this – why I'm – "

"It'll pay for your journey. Fair enough?"

And so that very evening I found myself going down to stay with our newest knight, Sir Mortimer Gussage, K.B.E., with a draft of his own obituary in my breast-pocket.

Tallboys was a place I had long been determined to visit: the house has given its name to the *de luxe* edition of his collected works where it is figured on the title page beyond its lime avenue in an almost impertinent perfection. I was under no illusion about the purpose of my invitation, nor for a moment did I suppose that Sir Mortimer would have asked me if I had not been able to mention at a party that I was doing a piece on him for his birthday. By lifting a finger Sir Mortimer could have met anyone in the kingdom. As an unimportant novel reviewer, my privilege had to be earned. And so it happened that, four days later, I found myself sliding into Salisbury station, descending with the misty October twilight, to be met among the churns on the long, cold platform by the great man's most finished masterpiece.

Laurian Gussage stepped forward and shook my hand. "You *are* Stephen Kemble? You *must* be! Daddy will be so pleased you have come." Her voice was low and crisp, her great eyes wide apart – a brownish green – her face rather round, above the grey Paris scarf, were it not for a high forehead from which the dark hair was swept back. She wore broad-waled blue corduroy trousers under a three-quarter-length camel coat and tried to seize my bag. We made our way through groups of clanking soldiers to a small closed Sunbeam Talbot and soon were driving over the river, past the cathedral and out along the Blandford road.

"I wonder what you'll make of Tallboys. Isn't it your first visit?"

"Who's going to be there?" I countered.

"Oh, it's just a family party for Daddy's birthday tomor-

row. There's Daddy and Cressida, that's my stepmother –
and Jane Sotheran – 'Sacharissa', you know."

"Gracious!"

"Don't let them both tear you to pieces."

"Are they so carnivorous?"

"Oh no! Not destructive. They just like young men. And
then there's Geoffrey 'Ginger' Bartlett – he's Daddy's publisher – and Hugh Curry Rivel, his oldest friend; he's a writer
too. And Julian Frere, who's a young Cambridge disciple
and supposed to be terribly clever, and that's the lot, except
for Norman and Mona."

"Who are they?"

"Norman and Mona Farran; they have the mill nearby but
they're always over at the house. Norman's another very
old friend of Daddy's and Mona does his letters and typing."

"Are they writers too?"

"Good heavens, no; Norman has a fruit farm."

"And you?"

"I'm trying to be a painter; I feel I've had enough of the
written word and 'la vie littéraire'."

"You think it's a bad life? I'm a would-be novelist, don't
forget."

She looked at me reflectively. "I don't think it's life at
all."

We had been twisting in the dark along roads which had
narrowed stealthily to lanes until at last we crossed a little
bridge and shot up a leafy drive while the headlights illumi-
nated a square brick house with a shell-shaped wooden
porch. As we drew up with a crunch of gravel and bruising
of rosemary, the front door swung open on to a bright
pine-panelled hall. While a foreign-looking manservant in a
wrinkled white jacket with a button missing was taking my
bag and coat away, Laurian pushed me into a large living-
room, where the whole alarming party stood assembled

round an open log fire. "I've brought you the new admirer, Daddy," and for the second time in my life I found myself shaking hands with the man whose work had changed it. A "humanist" is perhaps a discredited word, let us say rather – an illuminator, a life-enhancer, a priest-king or a poet in the original sense of "maker"; one who has tried to distil from his imagination an imperishable elixir for the unborn, the discriminating, and the lost. With his pointed bronze beard, his noble brow and piratical blue eyes, his vigorous nose and full rich mouth, by his whole buoyant air of ironical expectation, he suggested the High Renaissance, the man of action who was yet dedicated to poetry and learning, like Sir Fulke Greville of whom he had so understandingly written, Kenelm Digby, or Killigrew, made the subject of his only play. He gave me a warm hand-clasp and a smile of appreciation. "Good of you to come," he boomed. "I don't think you've met my wife."

"Mr. Kemble, your servant, sir." Cressida made me a little curtsey, her two brown arms gripping the pleats of her quilted skirt in a ballet dancer's gesture, and then she lifted her small nineteen-twentyish face up to mine. "Of course, I know all about you." Her voice was a tiny silver bell and every syllable blown out of her mouth like a smoke-ring. She took my arm just above the elbow in a light yet somehow clinging and over-intimate grip, and led me up to the haughty Sacharissa.

"How do you do!" Miss Sotheran's voice was deep and resonant and her greeting went down the scale like a dropped guitar. She, too, smiled and there was something I didn't quite like about that either, for she put out a hand from which all life had been withdrawn so that I appeared to be holding it up with a fearful familiarity.

"And now our merry gentlemen, God rest them," enunciated Cressida. "Mr. Bartlett, our publisher, let nothing him

8

dismay." I greeted an erect and shambling figure in a blue city suit with a large open porous face and flabby paw. "And Mr. Curry Rivel." A self-consciously "interesting" head with a swivelling Egyptian back to it, posed on the neck like an early photo of Rupert Brooke but shrivelled by the secret processes of middle age; dry lips, pale unfriendly eyes, sandy hair brushed back and whitening at the sides like wind-blown wheat, and a flying hand I seemed hardly to touch, while a high-pitched voice disposed of me by rising on the last syllable. "How do you DO!"

"Oh yes, Mr. Kemble, and I was nearly forgetting, here's someone of your own age to play with. This is Mr. Frere – Julian, behold another acolyte to swing the censer with you for the Knight of the Split Caesura."

A man in his early thirties, and so actually considerably older than me as was obvious to both of us, put down his evening paper. He was tall and almost good-looking; his face dark and intelligent but somehow slightly battered, like an "export reject" of a rather good design. He reminded me of a less suave and rather more *louche* counterpart of Senator McCarthy. "How do you do, Mr. Kemble. Of course I read your novel reviews."

"Yes?"

There was charm in his careless tone. "Or do my level best to: for like all young critics you seem to have forgotten Dr. Johnson – 'a horse that can count up to ten is a remarkable horse, not a remarkable mathematician'." He stuck out a long, grimy, close-bitten finger and pushed my cambric handkerchief further down the breast-pocket.

"I'll thank you not – " I began, but Sir Mortimer clapped his hands, standing erect with one leg slightly advanced like a bronze Aeginetan warrior. "Cocktails at last."

As they were being passed round by the dishevelled servant (I nearly said "house-boy"), the Norman Farrans arrived, and amid general greetings I was introduced to them. The one man present who was so original as not to write had a quiet face with fine, sad eyes and a mild, doggy look that went well with his old tweeds, while his wife, Mona Farran, was distinctly shabby; she wore coral earrings and there were lumps of grey in her short black hair; her green skirt was too high to my way of thinking and revealed woollen stockings twisted round the knee.

Sir Mortimer offered me a martini. "And how was London? Deliciously noisy, I expect, with Charles Morgan away. You'll find us abominably quiet here, I'm afraid. The recreation of North Wiltshire is the bottle, of South Wiltshire, dressing up. Here on the borderline between them, we seldom dress – not even *lederhosen* – and we don't drink – or at any rate not nearly as much as we should like to. And now, let us go in – Cressida!" He barked her name out in quite a different tone, like a command, and she made a little face at Mr. Curry Rivel as we began to shuffle towards the door, like sand in an hour-glass, all seeming to hold back yet one by one contriving to pass through.

The dining-room was large, high, and like the hall panelled in some pale wood; it looked unexpectedly formal for such an easy-going house – or was it so easy-going? For I noticed that the men were all in dark suits; even Norman Farran's tweed was a peaty black-brown Donegal, while the women, except for his wife, were in low dresses. Laurian too had changed into something white and was beside me again, glowing like a camellia. A glittering crystal chandelier was suspended above the oval Sheraton table where two branching cut-glass candlesticks sent out their wavering sprays. In the centre was a plain rose bowl from which a diminuendo of goblets radiated star-wise in the direction of each guest; we all had an old print with a glass top as a tablemat and even a written place-card. I dared to hope the heavy capitals were Laurian's, for I found myself put between her and Sir Mortimer.

"Most of us have to share a lady tonight," he said, "so I have given you the best of the bunch and penalised you with myself as your neighbour." His voice had a curious resonance; an irresistible voice in which something profoundly masculine seemed to struggle with an imperishable gaiety and charm; whatever he was saying, his tone made of it a treat, an enlightenment, a special occasion, while his laugh – a single deep, infectious "Ha" – was like the lifting of the cover from a silver entrée dish on a cold morning. I did not know how to reply and mumbled my embarrassment while I looked carefully around me. The table was like this:

I am interested in table arrangement; it belongs to a mummified world which I am too young to remember. I decided that these people must all be where they were for a particular reason. "Sacharissa" was famous enough to be on Sir Mortimer's right – and Cressida? She had given herself an important dud in "Ginger" Bartlett and a consolation

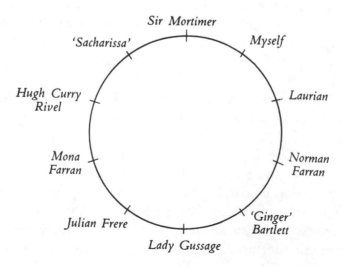

prize – clever Mr. Julian Frere. The two dim Farrans would presumably be fitted in last and so the one who seemed badly placed was Mr. Curry Rivel. Unless he was keen on "Sacharissa"? He did not look it. They were both middle-aged – she in the florid purple phases of the malady, he in the grip of alopecia, his main crop of hair receding at the temples, while eyebrows, ears and nostrils sent out a few last despairing shoots. I have always found it pays to regard any collection of people as enemies until they have been proved friendly, but I have learnt to conceal my suspicion. Say little; cast a cold eye; let them speak first and appear to take them at their own valuation – smile like a selective weed-killer – and in a few minutes most of the people one meets for the first time have irretrievably betrayed themselves. First impressions are best because they arise before we have allowed people to impose on us. Sacharissa – a mauve blancmange, I noted; Cressida – a marmoset with a chic suggestion of Saint Anthony's pig. Curry Rivel – a dried joss-stick; Bartlett – a randy major in the Pioneer Corps; Frere – a Third Programme barrow-boy; Laurian and Sir Mortimer – my only allies. Good – we were three against five – seven if one threw in the colourless Farrans. I thought of my favourite gangster, "Baby-Face" Floyd, snapped a smile on my face as one cocks a revolver, and waited the attack.

"I'm sure you don't know what is the hardest thing in the world to do," exclaimed Sir Mortimer, "especially if one is that despised thing, a perfectionist."

"To write a flawless page," I hazarded.

"To keep one's figure," boomed Sacharissa.

"To ripen, by natural means and in the open, a Doyenné de Comice pear." Hugh Curry Rivel's reedy civil servant's voice was precise, well-bred, Peacockian. "Taking your dictation, Sir Mortimer," rogued Mona Farran.

Laurian made no contribution and when I caught her eye she only giggled.

"A flawless page," went on Sir Mortimer, "I said the hardest thing in the world to do – I did not propose the impossible."

"Oh, what about *David and the Sibyl*, you old hypocrite? – a modest Merlin at his Table Round!"

"No, Sacharissa, I can tell you it's nothing to do with our art, though the Round Table comes into it. No, nothing so literary as that. It's just to give the perfect dinner – one in which everything comes off; the food, the wine, the china, the glass, the silver, the service, the guests – good talk, good fare, good people, good digestions. 'Dinner's everything,' as Hofmann wrote, '*C'est le but des actions humaines.*' They say food is a substitute for love. Well, it's certainly a bloody good one. Every night I think – well, perhaps this time tomorrow we shall have done it – and every time some little thing goes wrong."

"And tomorrow's your birthday!"

"Yes, this is the dress rehearsal for that supreme occasion, and who knows – it may turn out to have surpassed the feast!"

"Well, let's see first what we have in our nose-bag." Hugh Curry Rivel stretched out for the menu beside him in its white jade holder and handed it to Sacharissa, who intoned reverently:

CLEAR TURTLE SOUP

SOLE COLBERT

ROAST PARTRIDGE

HARICOTS VERTS   GAME CHIPS

CHEESE SOUFFLÉ

COX'S ORANGE   PITMASTON PINEAPPLE   IRISH PEACH
DOYENNÉ DE COMICE   KENTISH COBS

"Well, Fate has accepted your challenge, Hugh, the elusive pear is there!"

"Not Fate," cried Mona, "but my husband. We haven't a fruit farm for nothing – and you're right, they are difficult things to ripen. If Sir Mortimer didn't happen to be so fond of them, we'd never bother."

"I expect you find it a very dull menu," insisted my host, "but it had three advantages; it's easy to procure, it's foolproof to cook, and – this is a big and – it's the kind of unassuming sauce-free food that goes well with our wines. And in this house wine takes precedence. Let's see what we're drinking: with the turtle, an old Solera that was of age when Rimbaud and Verlaine played boy in Howland Street – a Montrachet, discreet as Docteur Blanche, to keep a flinty eye on the fish – a Romanée Saint Vivant as old as *Prufrock* that should hold your attention, Mr. Kemble – and when the birds are stomached and while the cheese soufflé exhales its brief 'Coronemus', the last – or almost the last – of my Yquem '21. *Reverentia!* And with the dessert we shall listen to the deplorable confessions of a magnum of dear Hugh Walpole's pink champagne."

"And you say this is only the dress rehearsal," I glamoured.

"And so therefore a most important occasion, a *répétition générale*. For tomorrow night I may still keep a few surprises. You will notice, for instance, that both hock and claret are absent from this evening's menu – and so are lobster and pheasant and *foie gras* and muscats and nectarines . . . If I weren't a writer, Mr. Kemble, I'd express myself through my collections, and if I didn't collect, I'd say it with claret, and if I couldn't get any claret, I'd long ago have toddled off to a better world. I thought also of perhaps trying to reproduce a typical menu from the Goncourt journals; you remember that turbot with the marvellous cream sauce which Flaubert served to them at Croisset the Easter before his apoplexy."

"Apoplexy!" whistled Curry Rivel. "I always understood it was a syphilitic seizure, not unconnected with his stomatitis."

"Surely we can leave it at epilepsy, a visitation of *le grand mal*, as the indiscreet Du Camp maintained," cried Sacharissa.

"Epilepsy – who falls for that? What about the purple mark Maupassant saw round his neck?"

"Proof positive," snapped Frere, "as Lenormant implies, that he had hanged himself in his bath. The niece and nephew had only just time to get the huge body into the bedroom. The whole thing was hushed up."

"I have a letter from Dumesnil," replied Sir Mortimer, "who spoke to the doctor who found him. He said it was undoubtedly what we should call a stroke."

"But since then Jean Pommier has discovered the letter to his brother in which he enquired about treatment for syphilis."

"Rustchuk Hanem? *De la littérature!*"

"Syphilis" – "Epilepsy" – "Suicide" – "Overeating!"

"Gentlemen – *mes enfants* – Sacharissa, desist I beg you – this is meant to be Morty's perfect dinner and you're turning it into a 'Crowner's Quest'."

"Cressida – your pardon."

"Naughty boy – and you're fifty-five tomorrow."

"Flaubert, Baudelaire, Baudelaire's brother, Maupassant, Maupassant's brother, Daudet – the badge of genius – they all had it." Rivel was still muttering.

I turned to the soup, aromatic with basil and calipee, which we had all allowed to get cold, and to the formidable Solera standing beside it. We were waited on by a trim parlour-maid and by the same manservant in his shrunken white jacket. And now it was delightful to concentrate on the little leathery soles involved in their lumps of parsley butter and on the gunmetal white Burgundy which went round with them. It was only then I had time to notice how unusual were all the accessories: spoons and forks were thinner in the waist than any I had seen and were marked on the stem with deep lions and whiskered leopards; everything glittered and tapered extravagantly; all around were china shells and pink and green baskets of china strawberries or bundles of asparagus and brown ducks whose backs were lids, and there was even a crackled china melon. The candlelight broke violet from the hanging lustres and was reflected in the glass chains which were looped across the double table candlesticks; our glasses were warm yet fragile, with thin stems and a pliant waxen transparency, in the centre the silver bowl was by contrast extremely severe and held some huge pink flowers that I had never seen before. Behind us on the sideboard were the fruit dishes; some of glass like moon-stained ice and others a part of some lustred shell service whose dishes were piled with apples and cobnuts, while in a kind of nautilus were three or four enormous pears.

"Where's the Pitmaston pineapple?" I said to Laurian.

"Oh, it's not a real pineapple. It's the name of an apple, a little honey-musk russet – so is the Irish peach – we're great apple connoisseurs here."

The visible world, I thought, with a vengeance!

She laughed. "Yes, we're connoisseurs of everything – 'nutty, compact and fertile', that's me. 'Aromatic, blushes pink, and a good cropper' – all things bright and beautiful, as long as no one else has got them – all creatures great and small, provided they're edible."

"I think you're perfectly right."

"Oh yes, so many do – not a shrimp is peeled without a

dissertation, not a sparrow falls to the ground without a post-mortem, not a gooseberry is taken without a permit."

"But in a way that's as it should be. To a great artist everything in life must be of equal importance – doesn't your father say somewhere that just as a straight line is really a number of infinitesimal points which we can't see, so a good life is a number of infinitesimal moments, but all equal in value, and each implying an act of choice. 'The theory of perpetual discrimination' he has called it. It's only the weak who think one moment or one point is more important than another."

Hugh Curry Rivel, I noticed, was listening intently. Sir Mortimer was still talking Goncourt to Sacharissa: "Then you would have been my George Sand," he was telling her.

Laurian grew more thoughtful. "But it's not exactly like that – for one thing some points on the line *must* be more important than others – the first and probably the last – and so it is with a human life – the two moments which start something and which end something are called birth and death, and all the connoisseurship and discrimination and 'hard gem-like flame-throwing' that goes on here seems to hush up and imprison a more real kind of living. We don't mention birth because it's so far behind or death because it's too close – and all this 'expertise' seems to me a diversion to retard the passage of time. I expect Canute became a terrific connoisseur of waves as he called on them one after another. Anyhow, it makes me glad not to live by a possession-clock, to have only a few sticks in my studio, a plastic teacup and an ironstone jug and basin."

"*Mademoiselle se croit trop artiste pour aimer les belles choses?*"

It was said with venomous distinctness. I glared across at Hugh Curry Rivel, who had sent over this unexpected volley, but couldn't concoct an answer. He held up his glass of burgundy to his nose, took a sip, rotated the glass with the base gripped between thumb and forefinger, and then swallowed a large mouthful. The wine was clear and bright as the red juice which oozed from my tender partridge's well-pronged flank. I took a swig myself and pressed my leg close to Laurian's to demonstrate my sympathy. I felt her long, hard thigh respond to mine, the knee-joints touching, and then my calf brushed against hers, as if our legs had suddenly been locked into position – even our ankles met. I was strangely disturbed and frightened.

We now appeared to have exhausted our amiability at this end of the table and so we turned to listen to the others like a jazz band making way for the rumba orchestra.

"Well, Cressida, it's all fixed," said Sir Mortimer, "my birthday treat tomorrow is to include both drinking and dressing up. A *soirée chez Magny* – a dinner from the Goncourt journal! Sacharissa insists that I myself impersonate Flaubert but I refuse unless she plays the maternal rôle of George Sand. Hugh, here, will be our liverish Edmond de Goncourt, and Julian, my disciple, the young Maupassant – 'Guy le chauve' – our 'green man'. Norman can be Alphonse Daudet (even he will have heard of 'Tartarin'), and our new guest, Mr. Kemble here, shall be young Zola. Cressida, you will have to play 'La Muse', Louise Colet, and you Ginger, our faithful publisher, Charpentier. Laurian and Mona can be the two ladies of my household."

"In fact your niece and mother."

"Thank you, Hugh."

"I'd rather be La Présidente than that odious Louise Colet," cried Cressida, "she had more chaps for one thing."

Lady Gussage gave a low laugh: I would almost have said a coarse chuckle, quite different from her usual silvery detonation.

"Well, we shall all have to drink a toast to '*notre grand Flau*'," said Curry Rivel, "in Goncourt's favourite '*cramant nature*'. I wonder, by the way, what the Hermit of Croisset would have thought of your knighthood. '*Les honneurs déshonorent, les titres dégradent,*' wasn't it?"

"He must have been a bit of a bourgeois," interrupted Julian, "or you couldn't call him '*notre grand Flau*', or even 'the Hermit of Croisset'. Imagine calling Baudelaire '*notre cher Bau*' – "

"Or Maupassant '*notre brave Mau*'," said Hugh, "or Daudet 'Dau' or Zola 'Zo' – "

"*Ma basta,*" piped Cressida, "let's enjoy tonight for once without *Le Petit Larousse*. And can't we have the dinner in a period when women were invited for their looks?"

"What about the Roman dinner?" said Julian. "The women only came in afterwards."

"All Roman dinners end up at Trimalchios," replied Sir Mortimer, "and I don't want to retire constantly to the Vomitorium or to have my coffin brought on by Angelo here" (he waved to the servant) "or to eat a quantity of stuffed livestock with liberated pigeons flying about the room, each with an *hors d'oeuvre* inside him like Japanese boxes. I always thought that meal lasted much too long."

"I know I should hate Roman cooking," said Sacharissa. "That horrible garum – what did Carême call it? '*Foncieré-ment lourde et sans finesse*'."

"Why not try one of their more specialised menus?" the sneering tone of Mr. Julian Frere took up. "Like the dinner '*en deuil*' Domitian gave his senators. You remember, Mortimer? The floor, the walls, and the ceiling of the room were black, so were the chairs, and the guests were introduced one by one during the night. Each found that a little column had been put in front of him, like those they set on tombs, on which his name was engraved, with a lamp like those they hung in sepulchres; then naked young slaves with blackened bodies stole like ghosts into the hall and danced ceremoniously round the guests before placing themselves at their feet; then they brought on the dingy little titbits which were offered to the dead, served on black plate. The senators were all expecting to have their throats cut and maintained complete silence while Domitian meandered on about the last murders and assassinations, until he sent them rumbling home with unfamiliar escorts, frozen with fear in their closed litters."

"I seem to remember he went on dispatching callers to them all through the small hours," said Curry Rivel, "who brought with a loud knocking first their silver columns, then their black plate, and then the slave who had waited on them, now washed and whitened, while each imperial present petrified them with further terror."

"Certainly."

"Well, I invite you all to dinner tomorrow, but I'm no Domitian," said Sir Mortimer. " *'Ego nolo Caesar esse.'* But what a writer old Suetonius was – that arid grammarian's style which always just avoids melodrama or bathos."

"Dion Cassius," muttered Frere.

"And what kind of Roman dinner could I tempt you with, Norman – a fruitarian orgy?"

The local green finger turned his sad spaniel eyes on his wife's employer. "Not just fruit – perhaps a few mushrooms – like Claudius."

"One mushroom wasn't it?" said Curry Rivel.

"One very big mushroom," answered Julian, " *'delectabile boletum'.*"

"What, you've read Suetonius too, Norman, in between chemical sprays!" laughed Sir Mortimer. "In the Loeb was it – or Bohn or Kelly?"

"Not Suetonius – only Robert Graves, in a Penguin." He spoke quietly, as if unaware that he was being made a butt.

"I don't believe we girls will have any more fun with

these Roman celebrations than in your stuffy old Goncourt,"
tinkled Cressida. "Can't we just have a delicious unassuming
modern birthday party with some slap and tickle and leave
it at that? Sacharissa?"

"*D'accord!*"

"Laurian?"

"*Double d'acc.*"

"Mona?"

"Most certainly!"

"Unless clever pretty Mr. Kemble has any original
notions?"

"Who? Me? Oh no, at least I don't think so."

"Well, let's leave the decision to our strong, silent publisher. Ginger what do you say?"

It was indeed the first time I had heard the sombre fellow
open his mouth. "The only dinner I ever attended which
came completely up to scratch," he said thickly, his false
teeth clicking briskly over the labials, "was one evening at
the old Algonquin." He began a rambling apologetic disqui-
sition in which, like a smothered fog-signal, one caught the
names of departed dollar-earners, literary wags, and pickled
punsters – all the glossy affluent nobodies who had flourished
while Sir Mortimer had slaved in obscurity at his *David and
the Sybil* or pondered those small works of art wherein the
formal pellucid brilliance of the twenties was irradiated by
an underlying unrest and dawning anxiety like the prelude
to the *Rheingold*. I remembered the prophetic ending of his
strange poem "Time to Go in":

> "*All the prawns in the sea choking in a glass jar,
> And summer strangled in a ruin of elms.*"

By contrast, the celebrities of Mr. Bartlett's story seemed
only to exist, like the publisher himself, when seeing off

the Fitzgeralds at Grand Central or playing poker with the Bromfields a day out from Nantucket. "Another remarkable occasion at the Savoy Grill, our English Algonquin," he went on, "where I saw the disastrous results of Rebecca's clam-chowder wager – gastronomically disastrous I mean, for as Heywood Broun cracked back to Bennett: 'It's not your liver, Arnold, I'm worried about, it's your circulation' – Ha! Ha!"

"*La table élégante est le dernier rayon de soleil qui caresse les vieillards*," whispered Sacharissa.

"Grimod?" said Curry Rivel.

"No, le Marquis de Cussy whom Baudelaire admired – or was that Custine?"

"I don't know – it's like Marmontel and Carmentelle."

"Pugin or Puget." They were off.

"Sénac de Meilhan and Maine de Biran."

"Orrery and Ossory."

"Condillac and Condorcet."

"Mahaffey and Cavaffy."

Laurian turned suddenly to me. "You told me you knew Sacharissa's books as well as Hugh's – were you being funny?"

"Not intentionally."

"I mean – have you ever read any?"

"Why, yes."

"And what do you think of them?"

"Curry Rivel seems to me precious, pedantic, sterile; Sacharissa sensible, flowing, earthy, dramatic, but somehow boring and vulgar. He's like the little fingernail rasping on a guitar, she's the flat palm twanging the bass – your father is – well – Segovia."

"You mean he combines them?"

"I mean that a book like *David and the Sybil* (I know one

should not go on as if it were the only one he has written), somehow unites the astringent erudition of Curry Rivel with the warmth and power of Sacharissa, and there's something else too, a kind of macabre insolence, like Julian Frere's conversation, only much more exquisite and graceful."

"Yes, I understand – and thank you. It's all there and even a touch of Norman's green finger. Autumnal sugar, country common sense."

"I suppose that's what we mean by genius, all the various little talents of an age amalgamating into something greater, a composite whole, a unique aroma."

'I heard the words 'unique aroma' from my young neighbour. Very appositely, for here we have precisely that." And Sir Mortimer shattered my word-picture as he filled the deepest and narrowest of the goblets with an amber ichor whose bouquet (how am I doing?) exhaled the sunshine of Southern Septembers strained through the faun's blown grape-skin.

Sir Mortimer raised his hand and blandly surveyed his guests. "Well – here it is. 1921. A good year, and a great summer; the first time one could go abroad after the last war but one, the beginning of the twenties: experiment, freedom, extravagance, hope. 'Teste David cum Sybilla,' as I was quoting then, and before 'solvet sæclum cum favilla' had become the writing on the wall. 'See fulfilled the prophet's warning / Heaven and earth in ashes burning.' And now of all that excess and promise, of all that liberty and laughter, of Capri and the Kurfürstendamm, Toulon and Montparnasse, Aldous's Crome Yellow; Firbank at the Tour Eiffel; Lytton's Queen Victoria; Valéry and Proust – we have only the gold from this bottle – and Tom Eliot of course – to still our gathering fear and the doubts which haunt us. Never mind! There are some young people here whose vintage is not yet gathered; may theirs be the outstanding one! Hugh! Norman!

Mona! Sacharissa! Ginger! Let us drink to those whose festival, as Leopardi said, is still before them. To my Cressida, who has yet to find her Troilus, to Laurian, to Julian who hasn't yet apostasised on his old friend, and to young Mr. Kemble here with his keen eye and virginal palate. Remember, young man, all I can tell you about life: beneath the comedy burns the tragedy; beneath the tragedy lies the ecstasy. The gaiety is in the gravity. You have only to dig."

"With a Hey, Nonny, Nonny," whispered the ill-mannered Curry Rivel.

They raised their glasses and drank with pompous cordiality like the Guardians in *The Cocktail Party*. Five of them now four of us, for Sacharissa, evidently sore about her age group, didn't seem anxious to collaborate.

Norman Farran grew suddenly vocal, "Reply, reply."

"Yes, Julian, you answer," from Hugh.

"Cressida, Cressida," from Ginger Bartlett.

"Laurian," from Norman.

"Mr. Kemble," chirped Mona, fiddling with a grey kiss-curl that had got into her glass.

The four young people nervously attacked the wobbling slabs of brown cheese soufflé which Angelo had set in front of them. There were purple wine-stains on his white sleeve – evidently another humanist.

"Reply, reply," chorused our elders.

"Give us a toast – a rule of life – a gnomic maxim," Sir Mortimer chided.

"My mind is a complete blank," fluted Cressida.

"Oh, Sacharissa, why aren't you with us?"

"When in doubt I try out all the last words of Roman emperors," said Hugh. "One always fits."

"Don't give them so much help, they're spoiled already," interrupted Sir Mortimer.

"Mine are Claudius's then," from Julian Frere. " '*Ut puto, concacavi me*' which I might translate: 'Goodness gracious, I've bogged in my bags.' "

"A toast, a toast." Laurian lifted a golden glass in her pale, firm hand. "Down the hatch!"

I was tongue-tied and Julian seemed to have said my say. The Roman emperors had deserted me.

Cressida stood up with all the artificial poise she invariably commanded. "Camera! Lights! Silence! I happen to think this is a serious moment; for the first time I drink as the wife of a knight as well as of a genius. As some of you may know, most of my youth has been passed in small repertory theatres, and to us a knight – except he of the Burning Pestle, which never came my way – was either Elizabethan – like Falstaff or Aguecheek – or Restoration, where I'm more at home. A sorry, shambling, sexy crew – Sir Lucius Bedwell, Sir Timothy Dildo, Sir Peregrine Pego – you all know the form. Even – dare I whisper it? – Lady Gussage sounds like a comic rôle to me, very different from fair Cressid. So I'm not sure if I'm as utterly thrilled by my elevation as I should like to be, though I'm woman enough to prefer it to being the wife of a C.H., an O.M., a P.C., and all those empty initials. So I'm not going to drink to the knighthood – and I'm not going to drink to the birthday, because that's for tomorrow night, and I'm not going to drink to Morty the Man – 'ancient person of my heart' – because I've other ways of showing what I think of him."

"With a Hey, Nonny, Nonny!"

"Sh – silence."

"So I drink to his books, to all his books, the Tallboys edition, and of course as well to Hugh and *his* books and Sacharissa and *hers* and to dear old 'Gingah' who publishes us all and so never can afford the newest Bentley, and to Mona who types him and Norman who supplies him with Vitamin C, but above all I drink to his new book, the work in progress – may we soon be allowed to read it, and when it comes out of the wind tunnel, may it belong specially to Julian and Laurian and Mr. Kemble and me as *David and the Sybil* and the rest belonged to Ginger, Sacharissa, Mona, and Hugh. *Compañeros!* 'The new book!' "

We all applauded and thumped and raised our glasses, now bubbling with old and faintly corky champagne. I gazed round the table. Sir Morty had never appeared so handsome; his face was full of colour, he resembled a dapper Pelasgic deity, a spruce, bearded Zeus, or the smiling, satisfied husband on an Etruscan tomb. Julian was looking a bit green. There were beads of sweat on his forehead, now covered by a limp black lock. Mona was giggling. Bartlett seemed rather blank, like a man who's walked into the wrong club, while Hugh was frowning over his glass. I looked at Laurian who winked her Botticelli eye at Sacharissa, who was gazing at Norman, even as Norman seemed to be far away, staring over my shoulder. I turned round and saw behind me on the wall a portrait of Laurian by Duncan Grant or Henry Lamb or some such period piece. I looked again; it was of a woman a few years older. I guessed at once. Her mother. It was a less happy, more sophisticated face, with the hair worn low upon the brow as in the twenties, the eyes lustrous and enigmatic, the lips slightly parted; a loose brown jumper and a huge pearl necklace merging with a brown county landscape; there were no pearls round Laurian's throbbing white neck – only moon stones.

"The book, the book," I shouted.

"Title please," said Cressida.

"Can't you give us the gen, sir," simpered Julian with mock humility.

"Pour it on, pour it on," cried Laurian, and Hugh murmured stupidly, "With a Hey, Nonny, Nonny!"

"I can't tell you much at this stage," went on Sir Mortimer, "but it's very good of all of you to take such an interest. I'm trying to do something rather complicated. An autobiography that's not written quite as one – more in the nature of La Bruyère's *Characters* – a few pages about all the people, all the situations, all the types, all the tangibles that have always so fascinated me throughout my life; the agents and reagents of my electuary. A home-made tarot pack as it were, of my influences; perhaps you could call it a bread-and-butter letter to the twentieth century. I've got only a working title so far, from one of the Roman Emperors again – 'Eyes, Look Your Last' – and I hope soon to find a better. I'm really trying to pass in review all the people and things to whom one day I shall most dread saying goodbye and to put them into focus, making each the subject of a prose poem – an Enigma Variation – round their attributes, like the Epistles of Horace set to the music of Pelléas and Mélisande; ancient gourmets like Ausonius and Archestratus; favourite philosophers like Democritus, Pythagoras, Aristippus, Lucretius, Berkeley and Hume (*le bon* David); playwrights like Congreve, dandies like Selwyn; beaux like Brummell; centenarians like Fontenelle and Xenophilus and Chevreuil; or people who lived at the right time like Rogers, Peacock, Luttrell and Lorenzo da Ponte or the photographer Nadar; painters like Altdorfer and Mabuse and Bosch and Patinir, Watteau, Fragonard, Liotard and La Tour; elegiac poets of all time from Theognis and Mimnermus, Tibullus, and Propertius to Baudelaire and Toulet; story-tellers from Apuleius to Villiers de L'Isle-Adam; travellers from Herodotus to Beckford; letter-writers from Cicero to Barbey D'Aurévilly, novelists from Petronius to Svevo; essayists from Horace and Montaigne to Landor and Hazlitt; and my favourite talkers and the beautiful women I have loved in literature, and their animals, Madame de Pompadour's 'Fidelité', Madame du Deffand's 'Tonton', Leonardo's lady with a

ferret (which is really a pine-marten); and the places, the
plants, the fruit, the china and furniture, the things one can
never have enough of, like Carione and Scarlatti, the stray
faces, the girl on the links at Carmel and the one on the Blue
train – everything, all my rich thievery 'bundled up into a
loose adieu', I've always felt that no one – not even Montaigne or Boswell or Gide – has carried egotism to the complete and final expression when, by sheer concentration it is
turned inside out and becomes its opposite. Ego into All.
Even Huysmans failed; he gave his arch egotist such bad
health that he couldn't reach the final. I, on the other hand,
may say I have never felt better. Yet I am carrying my
egotism to the point at which I'm about to pass the sense
barrier, which must be as dangerous as the speed of sound,
in order to come out on the other side with an affirmation
of the universal self in precipitate which will enable the
young and, I hope, the unborn to behold themselves, their
real destiny, their true personality, in a kind of magic mirror,
as I see you all in the crystal ball of this chandelier. So I
hope to come down to you, one day:

> 'Like that self-begotten bird
> In the Arabian woods embost
> That no second knows or third
> And lays e'erwhile a holocaust . . .' "

His voice was spell-binding as Casals's 'cello. We sat on in
silence, watching the sixteen candles gutter. "After all, what
a criminal thing it is that my Yquem can produce such an
effect when my prose cannot: yet one should be able to put
the very bouquet of all the summers one has enjoyed into
language, the 'pourriture noble' of the grapes, the October
glory of the mottled leaves, the weaving supplication of the
tendrils, the patch of brown spreading on the golden quince.

And that reminds me – I don't quite get all my vitamin C from Norman here – we still attempt a few freaks in the conservatory. Laurian, will you bring them in?"

She disappeared and quickly returned with a cut-glass dish of what looked like cheap cocktail sausages. "Here you are, Daddy – and, on top, my own special treat that I was keeping till tomorrow – a solitary passion fruit from the pride of the plant-house." I remarked a wrinkled purplish object like a decayed ping-pong ball.

"Splendid. I'd never even noticed it! I shall wait till I'm truly five and fifty and take it up to bed at midnight. Meanwhile, who will try an *Actinidia*? Norman, I'm sure you'd like a change from your régime of Cox and Worcester! You may have a green finger. Try one of my little brown thumbs!"

Norman seized the nasty furry creature and proceeded to skin it, revealing a blackish slime. "Are you sure they're ripe?"

"Ripe as we'll ever get them."

"What exactly are they?" I ventured.

"My pet plant – *Actinidia sinensis*, the Chinese gooseberry, as pretty a climber as you could wish and excellent in a cold-house, where *Passiflora edulis* is such a bad starter. 'Male and female created he them.' We've just a pair. Who's never had one?"

"I ate some last year," said Julian.

"Me too," said Cressida, "we'll share one this time!"

They started pulling at it like a cracker and Julian got the bigger half, which he managed to swallow. Cressida only nibbled hers and made a face. By now we were all sharing them, and pulling at them with our neighbour, Ginger and Norman, Mona with Hugh, Morty with Sacharissa, and Laurian with me. She won the larger half: I tasted mine, it was quite pleasant and, indeed, very like an insipid gooseberry, but better packed. Laurian was licking hers, as if it were an ice-cream cone, and her tongue came out like a pointed lizard flickering scarlet over the broken fruit. Something seemed to turn over inside me and I looked panic-stricken into her steady eyes, which matched the brown-green berry.

"That leaves one over for me to take to bed," laughed Sir Mortimer, as he placed it with his passion fruit and his Pitmaston russet. "A liberal '*en tout cas*' for birthday night-starvation. I've often thought with affection of the great fruit-eaters. Louis XIV always had a tableful beside him. You can see one in the big portrait in the Wallace Collection. And that Pope who died of eating too many of those little yellow figs – and poor Mussolini. Do you remember, Hugh, when Lina Waterfield went to interview him and he showed her his latest photos and asked her what she thought. Then he held one up and chuckled, '*Sempre più terribile* and how do I do it?' " ("Always more awe-inspiring," he translated for Mona.) "Then the Duce pointed to a basket and bellowed: '*Frutta, frutta, frutta!*' "

"Well, he wouldn't have marched to Rome on one of these," said Cressida, "he'd have fallen before you could say '*Dov'è la ritirata.*' " She rose and held her skirt wide as in a Velásquez, while all the women followed. Julian kept the door open, Sacharissa tacked out majestically under full canvas, Mona doggedly behind her, Laurian in her white satin sauntered off under protest, still munching an apple; and then the men closed round the decanter, which was parked in front of Hugh Curry Rivel. I now sat between him and Ginger Bartlett, Morty on his other side, then came Julian Frere and the fruit farmer. Hugh should by rights have passed me the port, instead he glared at me with distaste and turned away. "Morty," he drawled, "do you mind if I give you a backhander," and he slid the decanter over to him. I

was livid. "Yes," he continued, "you can't beat a red hock,
I always say, at the turn of the year."

Julian spilt the port as he helped himself, after Morty, who
then sent the decanter back in the proper direction, and I
poured out a glass with a concentration which was not lost
on my neighbour. Ginger looked uncomfortable, but filled
up his, and Norman took a very little, seeming sadder than
ever, while only Hugh appeared master of the situation. I
began to miss Laurian.

All the glow and warmth and promise had faded from the
scene. It was a city of the dead. The candles had grown long
black "thieves" which were dripping wax on to the polished
table; I was sitting in front of Cressida's array of half-emptied
glasses, which were all savaged with lipstick. Sacharissa, I
noticed, had put a cheap cigarette out in her finger-bowl and
another was stubbed into the remains of the *Actinidia*. Mona
had split the mustard with her cheese soufflé and left a pile
of blackened bread pellets, while someone else had buckled
their silver-gilt dessert fork on a home-grown pear. I felt
suddenly drowning, as if sinking desperately into an abyss
of lost identity after Curry Rivel's rudeness and Julian Frere's
hostile state. "Who are you?" I asked myself. "And who the
hell cares? Laurian, help, rescue, *au secours!*"

Then I looked up. She was there, smiling from her
mother's portrait, the round, dark, melting, Sir Peter Lely
face, the eyes veiled in compassionate intelligence. My lost
self found its way home. "Tell me, Mr. Curry Rivel," I
lobbed back, "used you to find a red hock any help as an
aphrodisiac?"

"My dear young man," he threatened, "don't you know
your 'Paneros'? The answer is there ain't no sich animal."

"What about yohimbine? Even Douglas admitted that."

"Certainly, Julian, but it is a dangerous drug which can
only be administered under medical supervision."

"I once read an ancient art of love," Sir Mortimer mediated, "which recommended only two cures – satyrion, whatever that is, and skirret, a herb which once flourished in our cottage gardens."

"Satyrion, my dear Morty, is an orchid," said Norman, "whose bulbs have always suggested testicles and hence potency to the old and foolish, and skirret, a Chinese plant which spread to Germany where it was much fancied by the ancient Romans. Skirret has long white roots, rather like parsnip, sweetish to the taste and faintly phallic. *Sias siarum.* You can probably get it from Bunyards."

"Geese are very fond of it."

"Ha! Geese! My book said that even to hold it in the hand reassembled the vital juices."

"Like an electric eel," said Julian.

"I've heard dear old Arnold Bennett say you can't beat oysters and champagne," volunteered Ginger Bartlett.

"You can't beat *anno domini* either," said Sir Mortimer.

"One consolation," went on Hugh, "is that we can only be stimulated at our age by what properly belongs to our libido. No more false starts, no barking up the wrong tree or ringing a stale doorbell."

"Ringing the wrong doorbell can sometimes be rather amusing," wheezed the publisher. "But I know what you mean. We can still keep a gel, but we can't expect her to be faithful."

"Suppose, Hugh, you are married, though," said Sir Mortimer.

"Then I'm sorry for you. For if at our age we will stand to attention only for our secret desires, then they are irregular verbs which are seldom to be conjugated in the marriage bed. Still, most wives have now so much on in side bets that they don't make such a fuss as they used. They hardly notice whether their husband is there or not. How would you like to have to make a public demonstration of your bedmanship, Sir Mortimer, with Cressida as your opponent in the centre court? That's what might have happened to you in your beloved seventeenth century, and I don't suppose a second helping of *Sias siarum* or satyrion would have been of much help."

We all stared at Curry Rivel and then at Sir Mortimer, who was spellbound. He gazed at Hugh with large wondering eyes that bulged slightly, so that one could see their profile sideways, like his daughter's; his mouth was slightly open and the tip of his tongue protruded. "Go on," he whispered, "what would have happened?"

Rivel stuck out a long, minatory forefinger. I noticed the tuft of reddish hair on the phalanx. "I will tell you." We all gulped some port. "But I can't tell you very much. It was called 'Le Congrès' and though it had been abolished by Justinian as unchristian the women seem to have got it put back in France about the middle of the sixteenth century. You remember that a marriage could be dissolved if the husband was shown through some defect in his equipment to be unfit for copulation and generation. Such as caused the divorce between the Emperor Lothair and his queen, Teutoberga. The smallness of the member, I believe, was in that case generally accepted as the obstacle. However, such malformations are infrequent and the object of the public congress was to present a husband accused by his wife of impotence with a chance to prove himself a man in front of some independent witnesses, usually the Bishop's steward and his ecclesiastical court. It met with considerable opposition and was described as simply a pretext for divorce thought up by lecherous ladies who had put the idea into the judges' heads, for only one man in a thousand can satisfy so sceptical an audience, and he would be an exhibitionist rather than a marvel of fecundity. During the hundred years while the Congress was reintroduced into France there was a great increase in the number of marriages thus dissolved, and so in 1677 the Parliament of Paris abolished it. The repeal arose from the case of René de Cordouan, Marquis de Langey, in 1659. He had been summoned by his first wife to prove his potency in public congress and had failed. By his next wife, Diane de Navailles, he had had seven children. Another Frenchman who failed in his congress before the episcopal court of Le Mans in 1655 was able afterwards to force his wife to produce their legitimate son and so obtained his acquittal. But I hope Cressida is not threatening you with such an ordeal," he went on, "for I don't believe it would cut any ice with a modern jury. If, however, you should fancy the experiment for its own sake, Morty, you couldn't do better than begin with a selected audience from around this table. You would feel among friends. I'm sure dear Cressida would accord you this concession, and even if we detected no deformity and you yet failed signally and publicly to perform your married obligations, you might still claim to have been bewitched, that some enemy had knotted a piece of wolf's tendon or cat skin with coloured thread while the priest was proclaiming '*ego vos jungo*' at your wedding; they had '*noué l'aiguilletto*', as it was called, and the only cure for that would be for you to urinate through your lady's wedding ring – which at our time of life, my dear Morty, is not as easy as it looks."

I found this monologue quite as repellent as much else that had shocked me since my arrival, but I also thought it of considerable interest, although no way to address a great man, and I was all the more surprised therefore when Julian Frere suddenly rose to his feet, clapped his hand over his wide clown's mouth and began to zigzag, snipe-like towards the door.

"My God!" yelled Sir Mortimer – for Julian, his free hand

34

thrust forward like a sleep-walker's, was working his way up to a china cabinet. "The Sèvres, the Sèvres," squeaked Mortimer.

In a flash Ginger Bartlett had grabbed him; he spun him round like a blindfolded figure and set him off on a straight course to the door. "That's the last of your tame Boswell, Morty. I'm afraid we shall have lost him for the rest of the evening. Mr. Kemble will have to deputise."

"You might at least apologise to Julian, Mr. Rivel," I put in, "you've shocked him to the core!"

"I think when you are more used to the ways of this house you will realise that it is the Tuke Holdsworth '20 to which he should have apologised for his '*non sum dignus*'."

"Thank you, Ginger," said Sir Mortimer. "As usual, we talk and you act – I haven't forgotten the evening when the Waterford punch bowl went. He has the most extraordinary cunning in this condition," said Sir Mortimer to me; "he can break the back of a rosewood chair simply by the angle he sits in it. An unconscious knowledge of tensile stresses. We have no punch bowl now, but a silver centre-piece – Cromwellian too, a real 'Ironside' – it can look after itself."

"What are the flowers in it?"

"I'm glad you asked; another little surprise for our local greenfingers. You behold the fabulous Egyptian lotus, or *Nelumbia negundo*, the sacred bean. For the perfect dinner party I need such flowers with no scent. Otherwise they might confuse the wine. They must also be large and firm yet not too tall and hold up well so that we can hear general conversation round my table, if so we choose, yet not see each other too easily. I'd rather look at them. And – why not? They should be unique. 'Human beans', as Pythagoras said. You grow them too?" He turned to Norman.

"No, I haven't the heat unfortunately."

"It's not just the heating. I don't believe they would stand commercial exploitation and a series of scalding inoculations and monthly sprayings from large chemical contraptions so that they might increase, enlarge, defy the blights and viruses and wasps, red spider and fungi, lose all quality and delicacy and bring in a sound three per cent in alternate years."

There was a distant noise of breaking glass and flushing toilets, a crash from the hall and women's voices. Sir Mortimer rose. "I think we should follow my young admirer's example and try to join the ladies, for I expect they are all in pieces."

As we left, Norman drew his host back into the dressing-room. Hugh and Ginger crossed the hall into the drawing-room and I found time to slip off to the lavatory in the hall which Julian had vacated. When I came back I passed the dining-room door and overheard Sir Mortimer in his old tone of authority. "Impossible, quite impossible."

"That is final?"

"Absolutely, my dear chap."

I hurried away as the door opened. I think it is wrong to eavesdrop, though it's different, of course, just to listen for a moment, in case it concerns oneself.

No sooner was I in the drawing-room than I made a bee-line for Laurian who was looking at a photograph album, but I had first to pass a narrow Regency sofa.

"Ah, Mr. Kemble – now you can tell us."

I found myself squeezed down between Cressida and Sacharissa. "Tell you what?"

"Why, all about yourself. How many questions will you answer?" As she spoke Sacharissa managed to make her words vibrate like the silence after Big Ben. Her expression held a contemptuous impertinence which seemed to strip me of all defences. She had only to say the word "Mr." to make me feel completely ridiculous.

Cressida took it up. "Will you promise – cross my heart

and swear – to answer six questions – three from each –
absolutely truthfully?"

"What's my reward?"

"You shall claim your reward when we know how you've
answered. It might be a surprise."

"All right," I agreed weakly. I always answer all questions
truthfully if only they'd known.

"But first, some coffee," said Cressida, "or I shall have
failed in my knightly duties. Black?"

"Thank you."

"One lump?"

"Two."

"Brandy or crème de menthe?"

"Neither, thank you."

"Cigarettes?"

"I'd rather have a chocolate."

She took one also and drew back her lips to bite it slowly
and neatly in two with her small white teeth. It meant, I
thought, "This is how I eat things. This is how I could eat
you. I am a dangerous animal" – except that, like everything
she did, it might have come out of some play. "Well, here
we go. Question one – how old are you?"

"Twenty-six."

Then from Sacharissa, "Two – are you married?"

"No."

"Have you got a mistress?"

"No."

"Are you a virgin?"

I looked at this large blooming woman with her mocking
expression. What should I say? I gazed into her dark eyes.
"Fortunately – yes."

She turned to Cressida. "Your witness."

"Are you queer?"

"Fortunately, no."

37

"Are you in love with Laurian?"

I felt like jelly. For a long moment I could not answer. Then I looked straight at her. "For a half an hour – until I met you – "

"And since you've met me?"

"Oh, Lady Gussage, that's the seventh question! I claim my reward."

"Quite right, *jeune homme*," said Sacharissa. 'What shall it be?"

"I'll sleep on it and let you know."

"All right – but answer one more question. What's your Christian name?"

"Stephen."

"Stephen – it would be!"

I felt like a child whom the wrong person has tickled.

Sir Mortimer appeared and offered me a thin cigar which I refused. I don't smoke myself and I find it a horrifying spectacle to watch normally civilised people turning into repressed maniacs as they cough and choke or clutch their pockets, interrupt each other's stories, pinch each other's matches, fill their own cases when no one is looking, and drop ash into cups and cushions or, worst of all, between the pages of books. But I prefer cigars. There are fewer of them. They smell nicer (non-smokers have a very keen sense of smell) and people are more careful where they deposit the ash. But not the stub, and I know of few filthier odours the next morning than an old cigar end soaked in coffee or brandy lying in a waste-paper basket by the bed. My mother was always singing a song about "a cigarette that bears the lipstick's traces", which seemed to me a catalogue of everything I disliked. How would Laurian pass the test? I went off to investigate. To my horror she was sitting with Mr. Frere, playing Halma.

38

"Feeling better?" I ventured.

He looked up, held his finger to his lips, tapped his head, hunched his shoulders over the board where the ridiculous little men were copulating with each other in intricate coloured tentacles, and waved me away.

Sir Mortimer patted me on the shoulder. "We're going off to have a rubber of bridge in my study – there'll be some drinks in a moment." He opened a door at the far end of the room and disappeared with Bartlett, Curry Rivel and Sacharissa.

I didn't feel like another *tête-à-tête* with either Cressida or the Farrans and so I tried the door at the opposite side. It opened into the conservatory. I switched on the light. It was a delightful place, a Regency addition to the house with one of those swinging bamboo sofas in the middle, some painted, palm-shaped, wrought-iron columns, and a variety of plants and creepers round the walls. I lay down on the sofa, rocked it gently, and let the cool air soothe my brow, which was fuming with jealousy and the Tuke Holdsworth. I knew my short life had reached a turning-point. In London my paper awaited me, the clean packet of crisp, fresh, bad novels, with the best plums already picked out, which was my weekly fare, the nosebag I had to eat through; the ever-present chance of some extra bit of work, an art exhibition, a trip to Paris or Bordeaux or Bâle or Aberdeen which was paid for by some cultural association or a group of wine merchants, anybody with a vested interest in claret or Burns or Bernoulli or Mérimée, perhaps even a *"rencontre intellectuelle"* at Geneva, a session of the European parliament at Strasbourg or, most prized of all, the Biennale at Venice. A chance of something to do, somewhere to go, when the married experts were too broke to take their wives. Then home to my rather superior boarding-house in Chelsea with the Italian cooking and the young men with a Foreign Office manner, my old school friend John Rainer on the floor below, my leafy attic looking over to Wren's hospital, my own novel to try to finish, the single Paul Klee drawing over the gas fire, the Tallboys Edition, complete, by my bed. This was the known world safe, if I chose, for another ten years, while beyond this door where I sat were the dragons, the *terra incognita*, the lovely inscrutable female animal at the Halma table. Should I press forward or withdraw? I thought of her mother's glance of reassurance from the portrait and of the wild leg which I had nearly tamed. Then I thought of wives and of women in general. Tears and screams and bad temper, girdles with empty stockings attached lying on chairs, lipstick, hair combings, tiny safety razors going drily over legs and arm-pits, false laughs into telephones, my mother's thin and angry face and my father's sneering tones. "My idea of hell, Isabel, would be to have to come to you for money."

"And mine, *dear*, to depend on *you* for sex."

Nymphonaggers! So that way Halma leads . . .

There was a footstep on the gravel; the outer door of the conservatory opened and Sir Mortimer strode in. He looked tired, white, and harrassed, and I hurried to explain that I myself had just stepped by to cool off. "How's the bridge?" I ended. "I suppose you are dummy."

"Bridge – ha! dummy," he repeated. "Yes, that is exactly what I am – you know something of gardening?"

"Nothing at all, I am afraid. What are all these?"

"Creepers and climbers mostly – I'm rather keen on them; so feeble and so aimless, yet they get exactly where they want; they rise by doodling: oh the cruel strength of the weak! They're not as alive as a good book, but they're certainly more alive than the average human 'bean' – this one in the tub here is a scented rhododendron, Lady Alice Fitzwilliam. The tub, by the way, is copied from those in the Orangerie at Versailles. This is delicate *Mandevilla suaveolens*, this is delicious *Hoya carnosa*, the wax plant with its brown bootlaces, and there is *Passiflora edulis*, the Brazilian passion flower that's suddenly laid an egg. Mustn't lose it by the way." He patted his pocket. "This is *Semele androgyne* from Tenerife – a rum beggar; this lot are some of the more particular clematis and jasmine, straight as a corkscrew, ruthless as a little woman. This is a *Lardizabala* – hasn't earned its keep yet – but I hope to eat that one day too. Here's a humdrum vine, Madresfield Court, a black muscat – nice plant and no mildew – here's a yellow wattle – mimosa to you – which Cressida's very fond of; and here, in this tank, the wonderful Sacred Lotus. Of course it's not really quite a cold-house, as when the drawing-room door's left open we can warm it up. We cheat, I'm afraid. But I like to tease poor Norman with his utilitarian outlook and his limited intelligence; all his fruit have such dreadful names, like 'Belle de Boskoop' and 'American Mother'. This one's a queer chap by the way. He must have come in as a seed with my 'cup-and-saucer' creeper here, *Cobaea scandens*. I thought he was a weed at first, but he soon got round me with those jolly red leaves. Nice habit too, and this year, after some scented white flowers last spring, he's sprouting berries."

It didn't look up to much to me. "Perhaps it's a castor-oil plant."

"Oh no, nothing so ordinary as that or we'd be using it for ordeals. There's a good subject for you by the way – ordeals of all nations – fire, water, the Calabat bean, the tanghin tree of Madagascar, the manchineel of the Carbis, the deadly upas under which condemned criminals were allowed to sleep. So simple – the innocent vomit, the guilty digest and die. There must be something to it. And here's my first and last love, *Daphne odora* – she's not much to look at now, but in February when there's so little else, she comes out in a tightly packed cluster of pale flowers with the most intense of all the jasmine, orange-blossom, viburnum type of scents. It's not an odour of spring, but one that defies winter and 'the sullen edicts of her mutinous season', and the more you smell it the deeper it recedes, layer within layer. Of course, it's tender, but it's August that kills them, not February. You don't smoke, I've noticed. No writer should. You'll keep a nose for these things. My young Boswell now," he tapped his cigar ash over the *Daphne*, "he believes that 'the road of excess leads to the palace of wisdom'. We used to call him 'the Dancing Don' until he danced his way out of a fellowship. And now something tells me I too shan't be able to rely on his services much longer. Perhaps some God has sent you to me in his place. You live by the will, I think, and you're too young to have been dominated by psychoanalysis. It's ruined poor Julian, ruined his health, his judgment, and his self-respect – and of course his vocabulary; he knows the answer before we can think of the question, he can't even dance now; it's become 'a compensatory play therapy'."

"But he still admires you, sir, I can see that. When Mr. Curry Rivel went too far in there, he was sick."

"Innocence upchucked! Well, I suppose you could put it like that – but never trust him. All admirers are alike. They want to get inside your skin and to have it they'll flay you alive."

"Oh, Sir Mortimer – I'm an admirer too."

"I suspect you want something else of mine."

"Yes, your style."

"Are you sure that's all? Well, I bequeath it to you. It's quite easy – a little oil in the vinegar, a little vinegar in the oil, and a clove of garlic rubbed round the bowl. It's not my style of course – Chateaubriand, Flaubert, Baudelaire, Huysmans – they all knew the secret. You must try to feel unpleasant things so truthfully that they become pleasant, and vice-versa. Laugh at the funeral, weep at the wedding. Remember we all carry in ourselves an inexhaustible source of vitality which is pure spirit. Art is the only vehicle which can hold and subjugate its burning activity. Life is unworthy of such fire; except at rare moments life drags us down. But art, alas, is for the few, for the lucky, for the lonely. Art is always round the corner. For the majority there is nothing but sex and money, money and sex, '*at nos vino scortisque demersi?*' And how they all hate art! Especially literature; and none of course hates it more than the literary – so remember: creation is its own reward. Creation – not the processing and packaging of what we have created – and it is our only pleasure and our only reward. After all, what's literature? An arrangement of vowels and consonants – that's poetry. And prose then? – an arrangement of consonants and vowels. There's nothing in the world so beautiful as one's next book or so bad as the last one. I divide people up into those who produce life and beauty and those who consume them, and when I have to make up my mind about someone, I always apply my test. Producers and Consumers – it sounds so simple. And I prefer producers who can't produce to consumers who are disguised as producers, the better to consume us. There are some of each here tonight; I wonder if you can tell them apart – you should learn to recognise the consumers by their vocabulary – it's more pretentious – they are nearly always rich or homosexual or both – the rich used to be patrons of art, now they are the artist's most jealous rivals. Three maladies I have lived to see destroy my world – or are they the same one? The increasing meanness of the rich, the ubiquitous infiltration of homosexuality, and everybody a snob about everything. And now I must get back to my rubber."

He went out by the garden door and made off towards

the study, which probably had a French window. I contemplated the "productive" vine in its October livery, rank and barnacled, mottled with mauve and crimson, still carrying one or two desiccated bunches of black grapes which drooped pathetically among the carefree exuberance of the "consuming" evergreens. I picked up a fallen leaf of the unknown plant and put it in my wallet. Then I felt cold again and opened the inner door to return to the fire.

Laurian made room for me beside her on the sofa. She smiled and then I understood that there can be moments at the beginning of a relationship when by a visual intuition the eyes pierce right through to the essential magic of another person, which is indeed the vitality of pure spirit. My jealousy had been groundless. I even tried to pass a little of my happiness on to poor Mona, who was by my other side. "Do you have to get up very early to fruit-farm?" I said.

"No, not very. But don't worry, we're leaving all the same."

"Oh, I didn't mean that."

Then Cressida drew me in to her conversation with the other two men. "I'm just describing the perfect dish, for the perfectionist's birthday," she trilled, "do listen – Stephen – Julian – Mona – Norman! Well, you take a large olive and stuff it with capers and anchovy, then soak it in pure olive oil and tuck it inside a beccafico – that's a little fig bunting – after cutting off its head and claws – the bird's I mean. Then you put the beccafico inside a nice fat ortolan, and after taking most of its bones out, as well as cutting off its claws and its head, you stuff the ortolan inside a nice fat juicy quail, straight off the vines, and you wrap a vine leaf round it – we can certainly manage that – and stuff it in a small plover. Put the plover, with a slice of very thin bacon round it inside a fine young partridge – if you can – and the partridge inside a lovely tender woodcock, well hung. And the woodcock, with a few croûtons of bread, inside a teal, and the teal, wrapped in bacon of course, inside a young guinea-fowl – they're too tough after the first year when they get their 'jugglers'. And the guinea-fowl inside a fine white Surrey chicken, and the chicken inside a capercailzie, very well hung indeed – that's always the hardest part – and the capercailzie inside a nice green goose – make sure its feet are still soft and its beak is flexible. And the goose inside a splendid Christmas turkey – and finally a real gourmet stuffs the turkey inside an enormous bustard – one used to see them in Hungary – and then you fill in all the gaps with Lyon chestnuts, sausage meat and stuffing. Next you put the whole thing in a large pot with onions pricked with cloves, ham chopped up very small, celery, mignonette (why mignonette? wait!), a 'bouquet garni', plenty of bacon, salt, pepper, spices, coriander, and a couple of cloves of garlic. Seal it up hermetically with pastry so that it's quite airtight. Then cook it very slowly for twenty-four hours on a gentle fire so that it gets the heat equally, preferably in the oven. Now, listen carefully – we're getting to the holy of holies of cooking! We have here the quintessence of forest, marsh. plain and farmyard, all these juices and emanations are being stealthily volatilised and united and blended into the most exquisite whole, a unique gastronomic experience – but meanwhile this quintessence has penetrated to the very heart of the whole matter, that is to the olive. So you carve open the bustard very carefully and throw it out of the window or give it to the dogs if you have any; same treatment for the turkey, the goose, the capercailzie, the chicken, the guinea-fowl, the teal, the woodcock, the partridge, the plover, the quail, the ortolan, the poor little beccafico, until finally in a spirit of true gratitude and admiration we serve dear old Morty up the olive. He will have to hold it for a long time in his mouth. I'm told it's *'vâchement succu . . .'* "

We all laughed, some louder than others, according to our sense of "*déjà lu*". I felt as if I had listened to a recital of the whole of Cressida's love-life, and she was still preening herself on her cleverness when the Farrans rose to bid us goodnight.

"Do come over to tea with us tomorrow," said Mona, "it's quite close, just the other side of the village, the old mill, you can't miss it. Now I must find my outer shoes."

Norman shook my hand with gentle persistence. "Yes, do come, if you can tear yourself away from all this magnificence. And bring Laurian."

They had just left when the bridge four appeared and pressed us all to whisky. I wanted to ask Curry Rivel a question. "Tell me," I said, "I've been thinking about what you told us. Did you ever *'nouer l'aiguillette'* yourself?"

"Good heavens no – well, not exactly, but when I lived in the Tarn I do remember a strange affair. There was a young chap whom I considered had been impertinent. He was just getting married to a maid of mine. As he left the villa I called out. 'That settles it, *je te nouerai l'aiguillette.*' I thought no more about it. But he did – and he believed it – and for a month he couldn't go to bed with his wife, and the harder he tried the worse it became, she grew more and more unco-operative; when he got into her bed his stomach would swell like a pumpkin and he could only obtain relief by keeping altogether out of her way. She, of course, began to loathe the sight of him. Naturally, I tried to make everything all right when she told me, but they wouldn't listen and made out to everyone I had bewitched them. In the end it was only cleared up by the priest by whom they had been married. Cock's testicles on broad beans broken under the bed are a cure (the ancient food of the dead incidentally), so be careful not to cross my path, young fellow!"

Suddenly everyone remembered the time and began to wish Sir Mortimer a happy birthday. Cressida made us all sing the doleful jingle. The great writer stood in the doorway as he accepted our congratulations, bidding us goodnight and looking slowly round at the china birds and the flowers and the bright fire, the Watteau and Tiepolo drawings and a pair of elongated figure-paintings by Marcellus Laroon. I thought I had never seen anyone so handsome, so compelling, with his Mediterranean figure, his warm and luminous personality dominating the room. He had a large red notebook under one arm and his plate of fruit in the other. He raised it above his head when he saw me and handed me the book to hold while he waved his other hand to the company. "Ah, goodnight, my young disciple. Remember my advice and steer clear of consumers. They'll gobble you up like they've gobbled me. Julian, you will show Mr. Kemble to his room, which is opposite yours, and you will treat him with the deference due to your successor, for your apprenticeship, I fear, is ending. I am afraid there is nothing more I can teach you. Go forth and prosper! But you – Stephen Kemble:

> 'But you, whom ev'ry Muse and Grace adorn
> Whom I foresee to better fortune born
> Be kind to my remains; and, oh, defend
> Against your judgement your departed friend!
> Let not th'insulting Foe my fame pursue
> But shade those laurels which descend to you.' "

It was spoken with such mellow and piercing sweetness that we all applauded. For a moment he still remained smiling in the doorway, a glowing bearded Wotan, his spear unshattered, while he performed a vague gesture of benediction over Laurian and Cressida with the raised fruit, and then he bowed to Sacharissa with his inscrutable expectant smile, seized his red notebook from me, and disappeared upstairs, his stooping, rather heavy back bunched into his wine-dark smoking jacket, a bald patch showing from behind like a pink celluloid duck's bottom clamped on his head, his chestnut hair a shade too long over his velvet collar. One could see nature had generally intended him to face his audience.

A moment afterwards Hugh solemnly offered his arm to Sacharissa, who also said goodnight to me. " 'Whom every Muse and every Grace adorn' – we shall see, we shall see." I noticed that she was taking a large whisky with her.

No sooner were they out of the room than Julian returned to life. "You heard that, Cressida – I've got the sack. The same old formula – nothing more we can teach you, we fear. You should find a wider scope for your activities outside the curriculum. Too old at thirty-three! Humanism is a club with an entrance fee of £2,000 a year." He clapped his hands and a skew-eyes smile froze his wide mouth, his long legs shot out sideways like Valentin le Desossé's, as with his white face glazed like a Rouault clown's, he trucked up to Cressida, firing his hand like a Sten-gun, then tap-danced a little, "broke" professionally, and whirled her off round the room. She too danced like a Degas ballerina, with her nubbly little legs, on their points, and her supple fingers cracking. They carried on an isolated dialogue between their personalities, she twirling and pirouetting and interpolating fragments of bolero, he beginning the Miller's Dance from *The Three-cornered Hat* and then bopping it up into a kind of expressionistic stomp, his dead-pan face with its lock of black hair sagging in front of him in a stylised rictus. Effective, I had to admit, though vulgar. I, too, would have liked to ask Laurian to dance, but I felt handicapped as there was no

48

music. Julian came to a stop with one of those fading cadenzas that we perform in our dreams, picked up Cressida, threw her over his shoulder, and carried her out of the room with one little leg outstretched, the other bent, and her arm held out with finger crooked, like a mechanical toy.

Laurian said, "I'd better show you to your room; I don't suppose anyone else will."

The house was very simply arranged, the pattern of hall with living-room leading into study on one side and dining-room leading into kitchen on the other was carried out on two floors; Cressida and Sir Mortimer were on either side of the stairhead, each with a bathroom, while Sacharissa and Hugh Curry Rivel, with a bathroom between them, looked out over the back. On the floor above were Laurian and her bathroom and Julian, and on the other Ginger Bartlett, another bathroom, myself. The Italian couple were in a built-on flat off the kitchen and were helped by two girls from the village during the day. The bathrooms had been made out of dressing-rooms and powder closets and in no way altered the architecture of the house.

A light came from under Sir Mortimer's door as we passed and another from my neighbour the publisher. I noticed with relief a fitted basin in my bedroom; I didn't want to wash in the bathroom between us until he was out of the way, for of all the visitors he was the one with whom I had established least contact, though some day he might prove the most useful.

"I hope you have everything," said Laurian.

I looked round at the pleasant white room with an electric fire burning, a pair of bird pictures by Simon Bussy, a caricature of Roger Fry, and a scribbled Lear landscape, at the single four-poster in plain mahogany with my white Egyptian cotton pyjamas neatly laid out, at the water carafe and biscuits by my bed and the little row of books, three or four volumes of Turgenev, a dozen old copies of *Life and Letters* and *Horizon*, *Wylder's Hand*, *Modern Love*, *Gryll Grange*, *Jacob's Room*, Francis Birrell's anthology of famous last words; I noticed the pale Samarkand rug, the heavy red curtains drawn across the mild October night, the glowing bedside lamp, and I knew that I had everything that I could possibly want. The room epitomised the enlightened pre-war comfort of which I realised I could never breathe enough; the security which now was out of nearly every reach, which once the addiction had taken root, one would almost commit murder to preserve. Indeed many people had killed Germans, Italians, Austrians, Hungarians, Japanese, just in order to keep it going, for to fight for one's country is to fight for one's standard of living, and if these things in themselves were not enough, there was Laurian standing beside me. "You need a *calm* mother" as my father once said. "A rock to jump off." It came over me that I hadn't felt quite so strongly about her since dinner. Something had broken the spell. It was another spell – her father's voice and perhaps more than a little bit of Cressida's. I was no longer obedient only to her low tones and direct gaze, but made restless by her father's words; his interest in me was breath-lessly exciting, but when I tried to think of that fine head which reflected the extraordinary Renaissance wholeness of his personality, I couldn't see him plainly either – only Cressida's body being carried out on Julian's shoulder, the rigid thigh, the bent brown arm.

"Thank you very much, for absolutely everything. Where are you?"

She led me across the passage and opened the door into an even warmer-looking room where I glimpsed a row of little silver gymkhana cups and a smaller sketch or painting of her mother. "Goodnight. Breakfast downstairs from nine onwards – dressing-gowns permitted," she said abruptly, and closed the door.

I have stayed too little in other people's houses not to find the nights very strange. When the guests are put away in their boxes till the morning and the theatre closed, there must be a simultaneous lifting of masks all over the house, a confrontation in the mirror of wrinkle and roll as memories and medicine bottles are brought out and the bray of one's own voice dies away. I wondered if I was going to have one of my own "blackouts" among these unfamiliar surroundings when one is conscious only of consciousness and absolutely of nothing else for an interminable second while the heart seems to stop. Then as I got into my bed I thought of all the other single visitors who had used it, their hopes and desires, their cumulative flatulence and indigestion, the worries they had tried to shut out between Saturday and Monday and to which they had inevitably to return. Tomorrow I must have a look at the visitors' book. These always fascinate me; I like to watch the self-assured signatures that turn up week after week suddenly falter and disappear as they get too old or ill or poor to be asked again, as the sociability is squeezed out of them, or as the genial host dies and the philistine heir takes his place. I like also to see the grand beginnings of a reign peter out into a string of poor relations and punctual toadies until the page begins to die a natural death and the guests' names are pencilled in afterwards because they can't be bothered to sign them, and the book itself starts on its downhill journey to the junk shop or the loft. All the windy pretension of a generation of noisy nobodies who turn up to stuff themselves every Christmas and suddenly conk out like the turkeys that were fattened for them or the bad champagne on their sour stomachs! Consumers, consumers disguised as producers – you should know them by their vocabulary: '*Couldn't* have enjoyed myself more – *couldn't* have been more agreeable – bless you, you *dear* people, thanks for a *wonderful* time." Then it came over me that in these houses they have a habit of taking one's clothes away to be brushed in the early morning so that when I get up I never can find the comb which I always carry. I jumped out of bed to turn out my pockets. There was my wallet, with the ten-shilling note I was going to leave as tip – consumer's conscience money – my return ticket, another pound and some silver, the leaf I had picked up; there was my nylon comb in its little case. And yet an absence was postulating itself. My God – where was the obituary? I went through all my pockets and three times over the breast-pocket where I seemed to remember having stuffed it. It might still be in my overcoat or it might have fallen out somewhere downstairs. I knew I should get no sleep till I found it. Supposing the servants swept it up tomorrow morning!

I put on my brown dressing-gown and red slippers and tiptoed out. All was quiet in the passage and there was a little light on the landing from a window above the stairs. When I came to the next floor, I listened. Silence. I crept on down, crossed the hall, went into the dining-room and turned on the light. There was a smell of apples, port, and stale cigar smoke. Some preliminary clearing-up had been done and there was no sign of any strip of paper beside my place. I went into the sitting-room, switched on a lamp, and looked in the sofa where I had been sitting. Not a trace. I was approaching the conservatory and my hand was on the door when I heard a laugh, a low sensual chuckle. Cressida! "Go on – admit it – he's a cross between a rabbit and a ferret." That was Julian's sleazy voice. The answer was another low laugh followed by a slap: the hollow dry detonation of a man's hand on a woman's naked buttock – and then no sound but the rhythmic metal creaking of the swinging garden sofa, groaning and sighing like rigging at night. I turned and ran.

Back in the hall I halted and went through my overcoat pockets with no success, and I was tiptoeing up the stairs again when I heard a door open. I shrank back against the wall. Sacharissa stood in the arch of her room, against the light; she was in a flowered and flowing nightgown, one hand was pressed against her chest. She looked absolutely ghastly. She had not just taken her make-up off, she had removed her mask as well. I saw a face haggard with calamity; lines round her neck, lines down from the ends of her mouth, lines on her brow, eyes staring out into some appalling vision with the grey opacity of dead oysters – a drawing of Lady Macbeth by Fuseli, a Regency Clytemnestra. She looked up and down the passage for a moment, then silently closed her door.

I continued my ascent and reached my room without incident, only breathing safely again when I was back in bed. Then the words hit me. "A cross between a rabbit and a ferret." Could he mean – would he dare? Again I jumped out of bed, turned on the light, and looked in the glass. My usual round face with the features which passports call "regular" – the blue eyes, curly hair, which has been untruthfully described as albino since my eyebrows and eyelashes are perfectly visible, and the small, tidy mouth – stared back at me. A face "*égal à soi-même*". No – he must be jealous of me to devise such an insult, and jealous because I had made a strong enough impression on her to give him cause. But the ignominious disloyalty of their relationship! – and under Sir Mortimer's own roof. Should I have opened the door! Should I tell him in the morning? Should I leave? He had relied on me – was it not my duty? I though again of that bestial laugh, the expanding thigh and the sofa creaking like a rowlock, and I was seized in a tumult of horror and fascination. If him, why not me?

Then I remembered the liberty he had taken when he pushed my handkerchief down. Could he have pulled the typescript out at the same time? Would I have put it in my breast-pocket? I began once more to mull over the proceedings at the office until I could no longer clearly remember anything. I tried to read, but even Turgenev seemed insipid. I ate my biscuits, drank my water, got out and looked for more books. I discovered a few old novels and then two of Sacharissa's wartime efforts. One was a horrible short-lived best-seller, *Diggory Dock, Smallholder*, in which a city clerk, when rejected for the Army, takes to the land, cultivates a few chalk acres with barley and Brussels-sprouts, captures a German parachutist, and marries a fascinating "*femme de lettres*" who is the widowed lady of the manor. I think the Ministry of Information must have distributed it. There were only thirty pages but they worked like pentathol.

I was woken by Laurian, fully dressed and very pale. "It is ten o'clock," she said. "I have come to tell you that Daddy had a stroke some time during the night and never recovered consciousness. He died about half an hour ago. The doctor is with him and wants to see you." She went out without looking at me and spoke from the door. "You had better wait in the dining-room. Angelo will pack for you."

In a few minutes I had dressed and shaved and was rushing downstairs. The dining-room was empty, but I detected a small, reproachful spirit of flame which still kept vigil over coffee and hot milk and also a poached egg and sausage in a covered dish, prepared before the blow had fallen. Since I seemed to be in some kind of disgrace I relapsed into the greedy, obstinate silence which I had found the best weapon against my parents and afterwards so useful at school and during my glimpse of the Army. It was a fresh country egg, the sausage was brown and crisp, the coffee delicious. I went on to a piece of toast and some bitter Oxford marmalade.

Laurian came in just as I had finished. "This is Doctor Hislop," she said.

The doctor was thin and sunburnt and looked more like Harley Street than Wiltshire, the type of coming man whose name is last on bulletins of royal illness. "This is a very bad business, Mr. Kemble. I will keep you no longer than is necessary. You knew Sir Mortimer well?"

"I only met him once before yesterday, at a cocktail party."

"He took a great fancy to you, I understand."

"I am very glad to hear it."

"He seemed to you in good health and spirits last night?"

"Perfectly. I thought he looked very well. Almost too well."

"What do you mean by that?"

"I mean he had a very high colour."

"When was that?"

"After dinner – and when he went to bed he was pale."

"You didn't see him afterwards?"

"Not at all."

"I see. Well, as you know, Sir Mortimer had a cerebral haemorrhage during the night. He was of course a hypertensive type, but such things are usually brought on at his age by a shock of some kind. Sometimes by over-exertion, sometimes by bad news, sometimes just by bad temper. This was found on his pillow. Do you recognise it?"

"Yes."

"You wrote it?"

"Yes."

"*More than anyone now living Sir Mortimer appreciated the*

55

things which he could touch or see – what on earth do you mean
by that?"

"I should have thought it was perfectly clear."

"Clear that you knew he was going to die when you wrote
it?"

"No. I mean it is an obituary such as every big newspaper
keeps in its files for celebrities."

"Then why did you bring it with you?"

"I had originally written it as a tribute for his birthday:
'Sir Mortimer Gussage. An appreciation'. My editor did not
require this and so he had altered the tenses. The changes in
the typescript are his. He will corroborate me if you will get
in touch with him."

"Then what induced you to show it to Sir Mortimer?"

"I never did anything of the kind. The paper disappeared
during the evening and I myself think it was stolen and
deliberately put in Sir Mortimer's possession by someone
who was jealous of me."

"Who so you mean?"

"Mr. Julian Frere."

"That's nonsense."

"No, I don't think it is," said Laurian. "Daddy said in
front of all of us that he accepted Mr. Kemble as a new
disciple instead of Julian."

"Well, I am afraid I shall have to keep this. I don't think
at present an inquest is necessary, Sir Mortimer's rages were
proverbial and I had been fearing something like this for the
last year or so. With a blood pressure of two hundred one
can't afford the larger emotions. But in case the authorities
should want to look at it, I shall seal it in this envelope here
– and may I have your address? I am afraid, Mr. Kemble,
that a most malicious error of taste and judgement must lie
heavy on your conscience for some years to come."

Angelo put his head in. "Signor's taxi here."

"You have taken advantage of the hospitality of a great and generous man to play an odious and dangerous practical joke on him, and even if it were through an accident that he came into the possession of this paper, I cannot absolve you from the discourtesy of bringing it into the house with such fatal consequences. You will understand that Lady Gussage is too upset to see you and that her other guests are not minded to. As her medical adviser as well as Sir Mortimer's, I must request you to go."

"Certainly. After the way I have been treated I have no wish to stay. I only ask you to show the same alacrity in getting rid of Mr. Frere, who has played this revolting trick on Sir Mortimer and myself. I shall of course consult my solicitors." I found myself replying in exactly the language derived from stormy scenes in Victorian novels, which he had already used to me and I felt a little better, for Laurian had been impressed. Then I remembered Angelo and put my hand in my pocket. I'd left all my money upstairs. "With your permission, I'm going up to fetch my wallet," I said. "I must have left it in the drawer by my bed. Don't wait, please. Goodbye, Laurian. Dr. Hislop, my compliments."

I raced on tiptoe up the stairs while they both remained just inside the dining-room. The money was where I'd left it and I was coming back through the silent house when I was seized with an inscrutable impulse. Why not? I had as much right, surely, as anyone. On the first-floor landing I paused, then quietly opened Sir Mortimer's door. There was no one in the room. I walked quickly over and raised the sheet. He lay in perfect repose with the strange emptiness of the dead. The eyes were closed, his pointed beard, sharp nose and waxen brow were like some painted Elizabethan effigy on a Cotswold tomb, while everything else in the room but his body seemed to pulsate with his indignant and infinitely lonely presence. His expression was withdrawn as if brooding on some unattainable epithet. Only the colour, a high suffused purple round the throat which contrasted with the pallor of the brow, reminded me of the description of Flaubert as viewed by Maupassant. I looked down at the noble head which had for so long spun the words that had created my only valid beliefs and on the one person in the house who didn't believe that I had tried to kill him, the first corpse I had ever seen – my "cold feary father" – then I dropped the sheet. I noticed the big red notebook by his bed and lifted the cover. "EYES, LOOK YOUR LAST", was printed on the fly-leaf in huge capitals. "A valediction" by Mortimer Gussage, and underneath he had written a quotation from Peacock, "Nothing in this world is perfect but the music of Mozart." I turned over the tawny hand-woven pages. They were all blank.

As I was leaving I glanced at the waste-paper basket. A familiar object reposed among the crumpled circulars, the empty husk of the solitary passion fruit, Laurian's birthday gift to her father. An appropriate souvenir! I picked it up and put it in my overcoat pocket. When I got back to the hall (my whole journey had taken only two or three minutes) she was waiting by the door. I noticed the visitors' book on the hall table and felt a wild desire to force it open and perpetuate my abbreviated visit: "Stephen Kemble. Saturday, Oct. 16th Sunday, Oct. 17th. 'The Sunday Recorder', Fleet St." – but no further delay was permissible.

Laurian spoke: "I waited to tell you that I believe you. I can't say any more. Goodbye. Thank you for coming."

"Please answer me one question. Who found him?"

"Cressida. She went in to see why he hadn't rung for breakfast; that was at half past nine. He was unconscious, but still breathing then; but he died before Dr. Hislop could get here. He is a Harley Street man who spends week-ends in the village."

"And my article?"

"She found it on the pillow."

"Could she have put it there?"

"She would never do such a thing. She adored Daddy."

"Had he eaten anything in the night?"

"Half a pear and the Pitmaston pippin; the remains were on his plate with his Chinese gooseberry, which he hadn't touched. He usually ate some fruit as soon as he got into bed. I suppose that was about one o'clock this morning."

I said nothing. I believe that even as I had apprehended her true self from a glance she had seen into mine. I went up close to her and put my hands on her shoulder. She raised her long, white face. We closed our eyes and let our two bowed foreheads touch, for a second or two, holding our hands together, fingers upward, palm against palm. I felt her sorrow, her solitude, her courage, her devotion to her father flowing into my heart. "Fairest Cordelia, that art most rich, being poor / most choice forsaken and most loved despised." I tried to put everything I had felt for father and daughter into the bone in my forehead. "I love you. I will wait for you. When I can help you, send for me," I telepathised through my head. I felt the faint pressure of her nipples firm on my chest as she leant against me.

We opened our eyes and were standing again on the wide stone steps by the blue tangle of rosemary. I gave Angelo his ten shillings. "Is Cressida taking it very badly?" I asked.

"She has been wonderful. So efficient. Sacharissa is more upset. There's so little for her to do, really – and she had a presentiment."

I got into the cab. "You know where to find me?"

"Yes."

We drove round the gravel sweep in front of the house

and then headed down the lime avenue which only a few hours ago I had seen for the first time. Laurian remained in the door with her arm raised in an antique farewell, and from all the concave unrestored panes in the Georgian windows I had the impression of staring eyes. I shrank back into my corner as the driver accelerated through the stone gates and turned down into the valley, swerving to avoid the two Farrans who were walking up to the house. She was red-eyed, holding a large handkerchief and dressed in black, he wore a black tie, this time with green tweeds, and looked straight ahead with an expression not so much of grief as of sheer and utter panic. "The few – the lucky and the lonely," as Sir Mortimer had called us – did not seem to include Mr. Diggory Dock.

PART II

Be Kind to My Remains

The days went by. My obituary was not used, for as the editor pointed out, names were what the paper wanted and it was fortunate in that a retired admiral of literary pretensions who had once been a Member of Parliament was in a position to write a piece. But my effort was not wholly in vain, for I heard Julian Frere speak on the Third Programme and his talk was repeated in the *Listener*. "When all is said and done, let's face it," he concluded in his culture-commando manner, "he could give points to the best of us. No one could so appreciate the things which we may touch or see – no one had so earned the right to say, like Gauthier, 'I am for the visible world'."

I read a good many other appreciations. I learnt that Sir Mortimer's first wife was called Lucretia Dunning and that she was the daughter of an industrialist, she had died in 1935 and he had married Cressida while she was playing at a repertory theatre in *The Revenger's Tragedy* in 1940. Her ambition had been to play Juliet, but since her marriage she had given up the stage. There was now a possibility of her returning to it. The funeral was a purely local affair and though many people went down from London I was too indignant to appear at a ceremony to which I still considered I should have been invited. I had had no word from Laurian and I would like to have taken refuge in my own work, erecting a wall of towers round myself as I used to in the nursery. I had wasted many hours in puzzling over the events of the brief visit and in trying to find a way of proving that Julian Frere had taken his revenge on me. Unfortunately since I had no idea when the obituary disappeared everybody in the party including the Farrans and Angelo might have had an equal opportunity to pick it up, read it, and deposit it in Sir Mortimer's bedroom. But only Julian had the motive. There was no more talk of an inquest. Dr. Hislop must have supported the wishes of the family. The will, I understood, had been quite straightforward: Lady Gussage was well provided for until Laurian's marriage and not altogether neglected afterwards; Geoffrey Bartlett and Hugh Curry Rivel were the literary executors, there were some small personal bequests to the Farrans and Sacharissa; and the *Dictionary of National Biography* to Julian Frere. I noticed but one odd fact. Many of the literary gossip columns began to talk of "Eyes, Look Your Last" as if the "valediction" was actually in a state to be soon published, there were hints that it was Sir Mortimer's greatest book but that it included some rather harsh judgements on eminent contemporaries and might have to come out in a two-guinea limited edition. Someone wrote an attack on perfectionists in one of the weeklies, accusing them of sterility, and Ginger Bartlett replied with a personal letter in which he cited Sir Mortimer as the exception, a man who combined the adventurous chivalry of the first Elizabethan age with the delight in skilled craftsmanship, the international vision, of the second. "Eyes, Look Your Last" he hinted would appear in the spring and the sneering critic of perfection would have to eat his words!

Meanwhile I reviewed more bad novels for the *Sunday Recorder* and in the evenings made progress with my own. It was the story of the childhood and adolescence of a young man whose parents were not at peace with themselves or their offspring, and of his gradual emancipation from them through his discovery of literature, in particular of his own identity – i.e. – (I suppose you will have guessed by now) through *David and the Sybil*.

My boarding-house was a pleasant place to work in, my Stowe friend who was studying child psychiatry was good company of an evening, I liked the Foreign Office young men and the stray colonials who came with introductions, the Italian cooking was good, the expanse of lawn and plane and pediment from my attic window both pleasing and proper. But there was no doubt I could not appreciate it as before. For one thing I missed Laurian, and I had tasted honeydew – the civilisation of Tallboys, the manna of humanism which made everything else seem either insipid or bitter. I missed Cressida too and there were nights when what I had overheard in the conservatory stirred me to a kind of frenzy. I took to following people who looked like her in the street, and once went as far as West Hammersmith after a stocky young actress whom I had noticed in a Chinese restaurant in Soho. Of course there was nothing I could say to her. "Excuse me, you remind me of someone whom I overheard being made love to." It was quite disgusting. I watched her let herself in to a basement flat, her pelt of black hair blowing over her yellow face under the scurrying light, and I set off home.

One evening after supper Sir Mortimer was mentioned in the boarding-house. My friend Bowles had read a piece about him by Grigson "in one of the several dozen magazines – you must read it. He hints that your idol was all wrong in his botany, had feet of clay, not of good fibrous loam."

"He spoke to me of flowers with great feeling, I am convinced he knew a lot about them."

"Well, read the article. It was a bit off the beam for me; not my subject."

"You might then move on to Douglas Cooper's piece on Sir Mortimer as an art connoisseur," added one of the Foreign Office young men. "He rates him lower than Sir Kenneth Clark. Would you believe it!"

"Well, he grew some very rare plants," I went on, "*Semele androgyne*" (the name had stuck) "*Actinidia sinensis* – and ripened it too – and *Daphne odora*."

"And lovely, lovely *Lady Althea frutey*," said the Foreign Office young man.

"Well, some I know were very rare. Look, I still have a leaf of one here." I produced my wallet and handed them the long thin ovoid reddish leaf.

"Excuse me, Mr. Kemble, may I have a look?" said Jock Van Breda, a South African visitor who was working in some museum. The others had finished with it and he studied the leaf a long time, then broke it at the edge and felt it. "I shouldn't advise you to keep this any longer, Mr. Kemble."

"Why on earth not?"

"You've never heard of winter sweet?"

"No, never."

"Well, there are two kinds, both found only in South Africa and sometimes grown elsewhere in greenhouses. This is the rarer one, *Acrokanthera venenata*, the Kalahari Bushman's poison."

"You mean it's really poisonous?"

"Very poisonous indeed. They tip their arrows with it. It will kill an elephant. The juice, of course, is obtained from the root, though the leaves would contain some too. It might well kill you to get even some from this leaf into a cut or a scratch."

"Did he tell you why he grew it?" asked Bowles.

"He did not even know what it was, or remember how he got the seeds."

"Well, if it's anywhere near the house and there are any children around," said Van Breda, "you ought to warn them. It's just as dangerous as the most poisonous mushroom."

Mushroom rang some sort of a bell – the bitter-sweet memory of the Tallboys dining-room – even as the leaf recalled my last talk with Sir Mortimer in the conservatory.

"Not quite," I replied, "since no one is likely to eat it."

"No – but all the same."

"Well, perhaps I shall warn them."

"Some of my children would jump at it," said Bowles, "cure them of all their phobias. How much would kill a father?"

"Any more vegetable samples from the house of mourning?" said the F. O. young man. "I'm rather enjoying the botany class!"

"Why, yes, I have a passion fruit."

"Good heavens, how sultry. May we have a look?"

"There's nothing to see. It's been eaten. But it was grown in this country." I rose and went to my ulster in the hall. The shrivelled husk, like a ruined gunmetal ping-pong ball, was still in my pocket. As an exhibit it produced less interest than the unknown leaf.

Bowles held it to his nose. "Funny thing," he said, "it doesn't smell of passion – or even of that horrible cocktail stuff. If anything it smells faintly medicinal to me. Where did you find it?"

"In a waste-paper basket."

"Well, I suppose whoever ate it threw it there in a rage. Even if it's home-grown it needn't be as nasty as all that. I'd no idea they were so astringent." He held it to his nose again. "If you let me keep it under my pillow, I might dream of this clinical aroma and locate it."

Van Breda now examined it. "He must have a lot of fuel to grow a thing like this."

"He said it was a cold-house."

"Well we don't get them much South of Durban. Are you sure he didn't just buy it at Fortnums and stick it on to his tree?"

"Well, no, not absolutely of course." I was really feeling less and less sure of anything.

The telephone rang. "It's for you," said our charming young landlady from the other sitting-room. I went into the hall. "A telegram for Mr. Kemble, reply paid. 'Can you come down for this week-end. Meet your same train. Lots to talk about. Cressida Gussage'." I accepted with the first lightening of heart since Sir Mortimer's death.

"A very good thing you're going," said my editor. "I should make them put your arrival in *The Times* if I were you."

"What for?"

"Only because half London thinks you practically murdered him. You realise you have hardly got a friend left."

"I never realised that I had a friend at all. It's a very over-worked expression. But where did you hear all this?"

"One goes to these publishers' cocktail parties."

"Did you ever meet a man called Frere at any of them?"

"He's always there, usually tight, fearful highbrow, I

hear he was drunk on the Third Programme the other night."

"They call him the Dancing Don."

"He does look rather Spanish."

"May I take this?"

"When's it out?"

"Next week."

"All right, but don't go over your seven hundred and fifty."

"If I can review eight novels in seven hundred and fifty words I can review nine."

'O.K."

I left the office with Sacarissa's latest extravaganza, *If I were Lord Lundy*.

In the train I had a look at it. It was no better written than *Diggory Dock, Smallholder* and yet I began to take a morbid interest in the fastidious millionaire eccentric who was also the last of his line, a receptacle, through his birth and fortune, of all the daydreams of those with whom he came in contact. " 'If I were Lord Lundy . . . But that's out of the question,' Simmetta murmured. 'And if you were Lady Lundy,' his voice was caressing, intimate, silken. 'Peregrine – you don't mean?' 'I mean every damnation word of it. There've been too many droughts and too few flowers these long ten years in Lundy Castle. Time it had a chatelaine.' 'If I were Lord Lundy,' she nestled up to him cosily, 'I'd sell the whole horrible haunted place to an American millionaire – lock, stock and barrel.' 'You're bang right, my very dear. He has.' "

Salisbury station once again, noisy with milk cans and soldiers but this time no Laurian. Only the ancient Daimler, the taxi which had been the vehicle of my explusion. The journey was darker and wetter and bleaker than before, the leaves had fallen from the limes, the square stone house had the sharp etched quality which English architecture takes on in the winter when the trees are bare. The driver's stooping back was divided from my compartment by a fixed glass windscreen. I studied the roll of fat above his collar, as conversation was impossible. I paid him seventeen and six-pence and rang the bell. Angelo appeared and took my bag again, then showed me straight into the living-room.

Cressida got up from a deep wing chair. "Mr. Kemble – Stephen. I'm so glad you could come." She wore a black velvet dinner dress which set off the creamy whiteness of her skin and seemed altogether more tragic and adult. "I'm afraid you'll find it all so different! Oh, you should have come to the funeral, it was so sad, so beautiful and yet somehow so right. Like something in Morty's own books. He always said that the three most moving things in our literature were the marriage service and the burial of the dead and – what was the other? Oh yes – the Yonghy Bonghy Bo –

" 'On the coast of Coromandel,' " she fluted. "Oh dear, I suppose I shouldn't. And yet, why not? Morty hated death. He used to say there were only two ways to look at it; as the most important thing in life, all one's life, or as nothing at all, a little fall in the dark on to the universal mattress. '*Supportons la vie qui est peu de chose*' (he loved Voltaire) '*et méprisons la mort qui n'est rien du tout.*' One should choose whichever attitude suited one's temperament, and he used to say that even if he practised dying all his life like a discalced Carmelite, he'd never be any good at it. 'It just isn't me.' He always believed the personality was extinguished alto-gether and that it was a very good thing too, that whatever we pretend to feel when someone is very ill, we really think 'Shove up and make room.' The proof is, he used to say, that we never really want the dead back. Never, never,

never. Do you think he was right, Stephen? It doesn't even seem to me as if he's gone yet."

"I know hardly anything about these matters. I should almost think he was trying to console you."

"In a way, he was. I used to be so jealous of Lucretia, that's Laurian's mother, his first wife. You'd have loved her, Stephen, she was so vivid, so impulsive, so beautiful."

"I'm sure I should."

"Everybody did – but this is all ancient history. You must be longing for a drink." She poured me out an acrid martini which had stood a little too long.

"Is there anyone else coming this evening?"

"Laurian is arriving tomorrow. She's been staying with a friend in Venice. No, I'm afraid tonight it's just the family."

"The family?"

"Ginger, Hugh and Sacharissa – Morty's oldest friends."

"When did they arrive?"

"They didn't arrive. They live here."

"What?"

"Didn't you know? At least Hugh and Sacharissa do and Ginger comes down nearly every week-end."

"Have they lived here for long?"

"Oh, it was a sort of war arrangement but it really started long before – well anyhow before my time."

"You mean they were all here when you married?"

"Yes, of course. Sacharissa's a wonderful housekeeper, you know. I couldn't live without her. And Hugh does all the flowers."

"And what about Mr. Julian Frere?"

"Oh, the poor boy's in disgrace – I'm not allowed to have him. Ginger's so certain he played that terrible trick on you. And Ginger's poor Morty's executor. I'm allowed to ask you down instead as a consolation. Let's look in at the plant-house."

We took our drinks over and she opened the door to the conservatory and switched on the light. "Mortimer said the Chleuch in Morocco have such wonderful gardens because they talk to the plants and tell them one by one when their master dies. Do you think we should tell these?"

"They look as if they know already."

There was indeed a more than autumnal miasma. The creepers were breaking loose from the wires and falling about the tubs, the vine drooped naked, the lotos tank was drying up, the Lady Alice Fitzwilliam shrank unwatered, the *Daphne odora* had shrivelled, while the poisonous wintersweet of the Kalahari Bushmen had vanished altogether.

Cressida gave the hammock a little push with her high-heeled black slippers. "Some nights when I'm hopelessly awake (you know, I suffer from pernicious insomnia) and I get too frightened by my own thoughts, I come down here and rock myself to sleep in this sofa-thing. It's such a yump-ity feeling – you can almost *hear* the plants growing. And the scent! And everything seems wholesome again. If you ever feel you can't sleep while you're here, I advise you to try it. It's never failed me – but you're too young to worry about anything like that."

"And so are you."

"Oh, no – I'm over thirty – and I worry so. I think of all the atom bombs the communists are burying all over the country, timed to go off when the war starts and now lying in left luggage offices and old barns and all the houseboats on the Thames. They say they've sent one round and round England as a redirected parcel which is always being for-warded from one station to another, and Salisbury is part of the circuit."

"It won't go off while I'm here. I promise you."

"Promise? Then I'll think of you when I can't sleep and that will reassure me. But oh – it's so terrible – the wickedness in the world – and because we in England are kinder and saner than anyone else we're in the greatest danger."

We went back into the sitting-room. All the "family" were there. Their greetings were noticeably warmer that on my first visit. "Ah, there you are!" boomed Geoffrey Bartlett and Curry Rivel allowed me, for what seemed an eternity, the full possession of his long limp hand. He wore a thick black band on his sleeve but was otherwise rather flamboyantly dressed in a very well-cut, wide-checked suit. Who did he remind me of? I guessed at once, for I had spent the last two hours with him. Lord Lundy. I couldn't see him taking a taxi from Newmarket to Tangier like his prototype on the grounds that both had belonged to Charles II, but I could see he was trying to look the part. His creator seemed the only one to betray any signs of grief as opposed to mourning. She was rather dishevelled, her cheeks were purple, her eyes over-made up, her hair untidy. Her satin dress flopped and bulged in unusual places. Her voice seemed less vibrant, her sophistication skin-deep. I complimented her on *If I were Lord Lundy* – "Oh, that!" she answered. "What good is that now?"

Dinner was a very different affair from the last. The food was good and the wine excellent, but there was no conversation. It was not just that Sir Mortimer was gone, with his ebullient vitality, or that we were all conscious of our loss: the impulse to compete, to show off and display our talents, was entirely lacking. How much the last meal had owed even to Julian Frere! I almost began to miss him – and to Hugh Curry Rivel who now sat there so glumly. Where were the boasts and the toasts, the unexpected alliances in the wars between the sexes, between the ages?

Somebody mentioned the Coronation and a faint interest

was shown. Hugh protested against the television of the ceremony and the allotting of seats to Canadians and Australians. "The Coronation is an ancient Anglo-Saxon ceremony, but in justice to the Plantagenets if anyone is to be invited it should be a few Norman French and perhaps one or two old families with the blood of the Valois and Hugh Capet. I like my rulers as Byzantine as possible; as brittle, painted and fainéant. I think of George V at a court ball during his jubilee, kilted and with rouged knees. I remember a doctor telling me that George VI had the most beautiful feet he had ever seen. Even the Windsors, the one time I had the honour to meet them, were like two exquisite figures by Kandler or Bustelli against the 'Bosky' of an open-air restaurant in Buda. I don't hold with royalty doing any of the ordinary things. If they do them properly, how vulgar – if badly, how pathetic!"

"You surely don't object to them owning race horses." said Geoffrey.

"No – there is a precedent for that – and I don't mind them getting drunk if they choose – but things like water-skiing, which exposes the royal person. That is what I object to."

"I'm sorry, but to me the whole thing's unreal. The monarchy ended with Anne as far as I am concerned. I don't recognise the Hanoverians."

"Who do you recognise, Sacharissa?"

"The Duke of Buccleuch, through Monmouth and the marriage of Charles II with Lucy Walter. You know his grandfather had the marriage certificate and destroyed it, as he told Queen Victoria, because it was a document which no subject ought to possess."

"They were never married," said Hugh indignantly. "It's not in the picture. And what about you, Cressida?" he went on.

"Well, I'm an Elizabethan – naturally. But you know who my other hero is."

Hugh turned to me. "We do. Lady Gussage, I should warn you, is an ardent Bevanite. Until it comes to doing without any of this." He waved his hand round the room.

"Dear Hugh can't forgive me for having a social conscience."

"I can't forgive Frere for introducing you to all those clever young men. Did you know Bevanites have more sex-appeal than any other political party, Kemble?"

"More than young Tories?"

"Much more – it's only old Tories who have any sex-appeal – ask any nursery home."

"What about old Anglo-Catholic fascists?" Cressida sounded delightfully casual. "Did you know they nearly took poor Hugh away to the Eighteen Bee Hive? It was his big thrill of the war!"

"Like 'Second Front Now' processions for Cressida."

"Children, children," said Sacharissa, "let's stick to the Coronation. Who do you think Princess Margaret ought to marry?"

"An American."

"A Frenchman".

"A Wittelsbach."

"A member of the Old Nobility and by old I mean pre-Reformation – a Howard, a Talbot, a Courtenay, a Stanley. Perhaps Lord Saye and Sele."

"Why not a Mowbrey or a Mohun?"

"A nice reliable Swiss."

"Why 'ought to marry'? Isn't she free to choose?"

"She should build a palace in Cairo and become the vice-reine of Africa," said Bartlett.

"The Queen must go down with the sinking ship. It's her

73

duty and privilege. Let her stay here. The Cabinet would do a bunk to Canada if I know anything about them, but in our crown colonies, mandates and protectorates, Kenya, Tanganyika, Nyasaland, Uganda and Rhodesia, we have the largest area directly under the sovereign anywhere on the globe. We must make it the centre of our civilisation, a new Byzantium since the west has become so vulnerable."

"One can see you haven't been there, Ginger."

"Oh, you've been everywhere, Hugh."

"If it wasn't for the Boers and the Kaffirs and the British I'd build Byzantium in Cape Colony," said Hugh. "It has wine and a charming climate. 'Constance' is mentioned in Baudelaire. Nairobi isn't'."

"The audiences are very good."

"Of course, Cressida – you've been there too."

"Yes, you forget! I am Duchess of Malfi still!"

"I don't believe they understood a word of it."

"Oh, yes, they're madly highbrow."

"What about Australia?"

"Too near the Chinese."

"And the Americas."

"Besides, Australia can never be central. Look at a map of the world. Africa is the central continent, Kenya is the centre of Africa, a few hours in a plane from the Mediterranean, from Johannesburg, from Bombay."

"Give me the Carmel valley," said Sacharissa "and the quail running through the pine-woods and the sound of the Pacific."

"I remember an outing of the Bohemian Club in the days when you couldn't get a bad meal in San Francisco," began Geoffrey, dropping his idea of the last stand in the Kenya redoubt, "when I tasted Abelone for the first time." And the conversation returned as usual to food but without any of the sparkle of the first occasion. The sheep were without a shepherd.

Suddenly Cressida and Sacharissa rose and left us and I was left alone with two men both old enough to be my father. The port circulated, with no backhander.

"Talking of tasting," said Curry Rivel, "I couldn't resist translating this the other day. An old Italian document in the form of a letter to the famous Ghibelline, Costtriccio Castriccani, Duke of Lucca. I'm surprised Pound hasn't netted it for the Cantos: 'Sublime Sovereign, I am the last scion of the famous family of Rotondi. In three years I have literally eaten up all the property that it took them three centuries to accumulate. Nothing is left to me of all this but an enormous pile of debts and a gigantic appetite and a total incapacity for any other form of exercise. I have a thick head, flabby arms, a heavy body, in fact even as your grace is all heart so I all stomach. It is in this capacity that I present myself. as the saviour of your person and your country.

" 'Your Highness has the honour to have been excommunicated. It's a signal honour in the eyes of history but a poor recommendation for the present. Italy abounds in fanatical rascals and nature in corrosive poisons. Your enemies would prefer to introduce death into your entrails by treachery than to risk an open assault on Pisa or Lucca. I and I alone can be your shield against these cowardly plans.

" 'My taste is so practised, my stomach lining so eminently analytical, that I am immediately advertised of the presence of the smallest quantity of mischievous matter. The number and extent of samples have no fears for me. I should perform my service in large doses at any hour of the day or night, not only at your table and that of the Duchess your wife, but at every meal of their Highnesses your children, and of anyone else who may be dear to you. In future behold without fear your cup-bearers, cooks and physicians, for I will be your Avant-Garde stomach and I am ready to poison myself in your service.

" 'There is another kind of danger to which great hearts are exposed. Ever since arrogant Diomede wounded Venus, the Goddess has taken vengeance on poor mortals. I don't refer to those metaphorical injuries which the Poets make us yawn over, but those miserable girls who devour a hero to the point of total dissolution. Very well. I will be your torch-bearer in this dark conflict, whether a new road is to be opened or an old one reconnoitred – only Your Highness must give me twenty-four hours' warning by your Almoner or the Captain of the Guard.

" 'When Your Majesty is in good health, I shall take my wages in the form of the foods I taste, but to satiety, but when, in the natural order of things, cooks give way to doctors, I shall not hesitate to sample all their remedies, internal or external. But I shall expect to be paid then in money. The valuation shall be made according to the ordinance of the Emperor Maximin, such as History reports it, i.e. forty pounds of meat and twenty-eight pints of wine a day. I think to choose an Emperor's stomach as a measure of capacity is the worthiest hommage that good Ghibellines like you and me can pay to the imperial dignity.

" 'It only remains to settle a tariff for my secret services. Such intimate functions cannot be rewarded only with gold. A warrior is not less brave who enters a besieged town through the sewer. And so I ask of Your Highness the first estates he shall seize to be erected into a marquisate, with the command of the *condottiere* and the office of super-intendent.

" 'I shall not cease, Sublime Sovereign, to address to heaven my prayers for the preservation of my life, which will also be yours,

Gianbattista Rotondi.'

In the margin was written 'accepted'."

"Charming," said Bartlett. "How Morty would have loved that. What do you think, Kemble?"

"I should have thought it would have bored him stiff." There was a moment of consternation and the two elderly gentlemen caught each other's eye. "I don't know where you got it," I went on, "but there's nothing genuine about that. Thirteen hundred or so was Castriccani's date and there was little or no syphilis then or boring love poetry either – it probably comes from Machiavelli's life of him. Where did you find it?"

Curry Rivel did not seem at all put out. "In the cooking almanac of Grimod de La Reynière."

"You should consult original sources."

"I refrain from the pun," he bowed, "and I am delighted to stand corrected before one in whom Sir Mortimer had so much confidence."

"I wouldn't have trusted that man a yard," said Bartlett. "He's thinking only of his salary."

The port came round again. I refused it.

"Ah yes – but he was in a hopeless spot – and think how many people have been poisoned," answered Rivel. "More than we shall ever know. So you've read history, Mr. Kemble? I took that school."

"You were at Oxford with Sir Mortimer, weren't you?"

"He was at Balliol, I was at Merton. Ginger here was at Queens."

"What – all at the same time?"

"And Norman too – at Worcester."

"Yes – all four of us," said Ginger. "It takes one back."

"If one's willing to go," I murmured.

"And now we are only three," said Curry Rivel. "I always thought that Morty would live to bury us all."

"His fame will do that."

"I hope so with all my heart. But what is fame these days? As Mr. Salteena said – 'piffle before the wind'. Literature is a dying art – dying of neglect. Nobody reads any more. Critics continue to be paid by a few newspapers and academic institutions because they are behind the times: they assume the public still want book reviews although they don't want books. They may be right, the habit dies hard. You should review imaginary novels: you'd make a name for yourself."

"Yes – as a publisher, alas, I'm with you. As Jack Priestley said the other day, best-sellers aren't written by writers any more, but by fellows on rafts or on the top of Everest or at the bottom of the sea, and they can only write one each. And the Past, that's no good at all – reprints. The most dismal word in the language. We can't afford to publish any more unless we can serialise – and you know what the Sunday papers want. Well, thank God, I published Gussage when the going was good. I shall have my niche for that."

"Don't forget you published 'Curry Rivel' too."

"Ah yes, Hugh – we had an enquiry for one of your books the other day, a copy of *Muscat and Mountain* for Australia."

"A travel book?" I ventured.

"No, something of an *olla podrida*, a *cotignac* of out-of-the-way information, called after our old dessert wines. And if I may say so – just what they need 'down under'."

"They seem to think so too. It's not the first time they've asked by any means."

"It's twenty years since that book came out and I still get a statement every year."

"And how about *If I were Lord Lundy*," I hazarded.

"Ah – Sacharissa – she's a different proposition – serial rights, film rights, broadcasting – you never know what's going to bob up with her. She pulps like a grapefruit. *Dig-*

gory-Dock, Smallholder best thing since Farnol – and *The Scoop in Our Shelter* – do you know there's still a demand for that, seven years after the war?"

"A pamphlet about the Gibraltarians in London," explained Curry Rivel.

"Very touching."

"And when is 'Eyes, Look Your Last' coming out?"

"Ah, my young friend, that is what I wanted to talk to you about. There's a book, a great book; I said to Morty when I saw it: 'Morty, old boy – there's nothing now between you and the Nobel Prize.' 'Except my translators,' he cracked back."

"It was finished then?"

"Finished, I would say, but unrevised. And that meant with Morty – hardly begun. He would give a book three or four coats of paint as he used to say. Revise the manuscript, have it typed, revise the typescript, have it retyped, revise that, have it in proof, revise the proofs, get the page proofs, delete insertions and insert deletions; sometimes the whole book had to be reset. I'll never forget the time we forgot to let him revise an 'errata' slip 'for I'm a Peacockian' read 'I'm a Leacockian' instead of the other way round. Now his last book is almost unrevised and I somehow feel, as his literary executor, that he would have wanted you, Kemble, to revise it. He cared so much for the young."

"With a Hey Nonny Nonny."

"My dear Hugh – of course you can't have his knowledge, his imagination or his taste – but you have a right to say 'I'm bored' – 'this part's not so good' – 'I don't know what he's talking about' – or just 'Bravo – bis, bis.' "

"So many allusions of his," interrupted Hugh, "require a fund of common knowledge to which your generation seems unable to subscribe. *Ubi sapientiae cultissima via.* I met a young person the other day who did not even know that

Cherubino and his love for the Countess was taken from the episode of Petit-Louis, the teen-age music teacher of the Duchesse de Choiseul – how can anyone enjoy *Figaro* if they think it's about Spain? *Qué barbaridad!* That hot summer day on the Loire, the huge chateau, the pagoda of friendship in the distance, the blue haze of the forest, the splendid company, the great Duke wearing the Pompadour's rose diamond in his Golden Fleece and walking with his mistress, Madame de Brionne or his proud sister, the Duchesse de Grammont, while his beautiful virtuous devoted wife tries to divert herself with the boy prodigy who teaches her the *clareçin*, ready to throw himself in the Loire for love, and the adoring Abbé Barthélemy (the young Anarcharsis) whom she was to save from the guillotine – it's all pure Fragonard – ah Chanteloup – Chanteloup – what would I not give for an evening there – and what wouldn't Mozart, I suspect! Figaro was a 'philosopher' of course, a Diderot young man, and I expect one touch here on some scandal about his birth like D'Alembert's, with which Beaumarchais was familiar – Almaviva – living heart – the living heart of the rococo of course, the golden age which Mozart had known as a child, when he played in the salon of the Prince de Conti (you know the picture?) and to which he now bids such exquisite farewell – ah Chanteloup, *cantus lupi*, winter wolf-song in the forest of Amboise – and to think there are still people who prefer *Don Giovanni!*"

"I do, for one."

"My poor young friend – marble guests and paranoid seducers – it's half-way to Wagner!"

"I like *Götterdammerung* best of all."

"Brünnhilde and Siegfried, love among the beech-nuts, old man Wotan-Gunther and the Gibichungs – what a set! And the orchestra with its thousand 'I told you so's'."

"Very entertaining," scowled Bartlett, "but we are listening to the living, Hugh, I would rather converse with the dead. What is your answer, Mr. Kemble?"

"I'd like to see the book first; I mean, I don't think I'm in the least qualified."

"I'm afraid the original manuscript is far too precious to leave my possession and I wouldn't like the typescript to go out of this house. But of course we are in a great hurry, we shall arrange something. What do you say?"

"I repeat, I'm willing to try but I must see the book first."

"Better still," said Curry Rivel, "Cressida shall read it to you."

We rose and filed to the drawing-room. Cressida and Sacharissa were at the halma board. "Such a sweet game," she said, "so constructive – one can't lose one's temper."

"I don't wish to interrupt," said Bartlett, "but I think it's time you read us a little of Morty's book."

"I don't think I could – and besides his writing is so masculine – I'd much rather Hugh did. He reads so beautifully."

"No, Cressida, remember he said it was your book, it was for you he quoted Troilus:

> *'Injurious time now with a robber's haste*
> *Crams his rich thievery up, he knows not how:*
> *As many farewells as be stars in heaven*
> *With distinct breath and consign'd kisses to them,*
> *He fumbles up into a loose adieu – ' "*

There was silence, then Cressida finished the quotation almost inaudibly:

> *"And scants us with a single famish'd kiss*
> *Distasted with the salt of broken tears."*

"I'll go and get the manuscript," said the publisher Geoffrey. He disappeared upstairs as Angelo brought in the coffee. The cups were lilac and gold, with a border of fuchsias round the rim, and the coffee was in a little silver gilt jug with the handle sticking out at right-angles. It was very good coffee and the brown sugar was like uncut diamonds. Cigars were passed again and Sacharissa took one. Hugh settled himself into what I supposed had been Sir Mortimer's favourite chair just as Bartlett returned with an important-looking folder which he handed to Cressida. It was not the red notebook I had seen, and seemed to contain a wad of typescript.

Cressida cleared her throat and looked round at us with sweet sad eyes. She opened the book and began to read with crystal reverence. " 'Eyes, look your last. A valediction against mourning.

" 'Oh the emptiness of middle-age, when desire dwindles and hope falters, when we turn from addition to subtraction, multiplication to long division, when death grows nearer but only near enough to point the pointlessness of life and youth withdraws so fast that it seems to have always belonged to someone else. The middle-aged are like a roomful of clocks ticking briskly away, striking in uncommunicating union, yet clocks with a memory, clocks that falter before they chime, and which have a way of stopping when we are not looking.

" 'And memory – those memories which we boast can never be taken from us! If you should swim in the lake of Annecy and look down through the blue water you will notice the waterweed, white blossoms a yard or so under, all aspiring towards the air and each on a single pale stem which goes down, down, until it disappears in the dark with a suggestion of loneliness and infinity, as if the flowers are kites flown from the underworld. One can seize these slimy bell-ropes and pull up twenty or thirty feet of them, suffocation of sad separateness – so it is with the memories of the middle-aged. A moment's pause to reflect and we are entangled with the fragile invisible roots, which stretch down for ever in meaningless profusion and come away in our hand. And no matter where we begin, we are at the wrong end of the beanstalk and brought nearer to despair: beneath the happiest moment lies the human predicament, the foreknowledge to which the fore-brain dooms us.

" 'The young are busy growing into life, growing into the relationships with each other, finding their feet; the old know that there is no intimacy, no tie however close of love or habit, which is not, despite appearances, pathetically and monstrously untrue. Unutterably separate and apart the bright clocks stand side by side keeping time to the same minute. World without hope. Amen.

" 'Each moment in human life, however frivolous and inconsequent, becomes tragic when related to any other. Tragedy is the human dimension, it is what is present in a lock of hair and absent from a fossil or the bark of a tree. And so to remember is to ensadden, the echo of the loudest laughter is a sigh.' "

There was an extraordinary commotion, and with a terrible choking cough, her hair falling over her purple face, her chewed cigar-butt in her hand, Sacharissa ran sobbing from the room.

Curry Rivel jumped up. "Shall I go after her?"

Cressida put the book down. "I shan't read another word. I think it was a horrible idea. We'll both go."

As they left Bartlett took the typescript. "What a pity. It begins to get so good and not at all depressing." He read the next sentence: " 'It is then and only then we learn that it is not love which makes life bearable but time, the brain ripens before it rots and even if we are not artists, our memories make works of art from the raw material of the present, for from our lives macerated in time we desire the poetry of loving, the aroma of transience.

> " 'Parthenophil is lost and I would seek him
> For he is like to something I remember
> A great while since: a long long time ago.'

And now how about a whisky and soda?" He poured it out into a heavy hob-nailed glass as the others returned.

"Sacharissa's too upset – she's gone to bed," said Cressida.

"And what did you think of it, Kemble?" said Curry Rivel.

"I have no fault to find."

"So far, so good in fact – and do you think that will be the verdict of your whole generation of baby-faced killers?"

"I'm afraid I can't answer for them."

"But you will help us a little with the rest?"

"I don't think it's in the least necessary."

"It's a matter of deciding which characters in the valediction he could have left in; we must anticipate his fastidiousness if that were possible."

"Oh do stop talking about Morty and his book for one moment," interrupted Cressida. "It's becoming morbid."

"Yes, yes," said Hugh, "*Il faut tenter de vivre* Geoffrey, get us something lively on the wireless."

The publisher's large hand turned a switch by a built-in panel. "Morty arranged this," he said, "because a radio shouldn't be listened to unless it's invisible."

There was a click and a buzz and a ripple of suave consumer tones: "And so, when the question posed itself at

Geneva: precisely what contemporary English author could we acclaim as of European significance, I replied without hesitation: 'Mortimer Gussage.' Here is strength with sweetness, the *perpetum mobile* of the solitary mind in both patristic and phenomenological isolation, immanently aware of both methodology and madness. Arksakov; Goncharov; Berdiaev; Chestov; Rumpelmayer here in fact as well as in intention with Notker; Novalis; Goldprick; Mittersill; Babinsky and Bouth, and so permit contemporary man to escape his elenchy and choose his querencia following as it were the amber light for Paddington without ever for a moment losing sight of the green for Waterloo." And then another voice: "You have just been listening to a report on European cultural exchanges by Mr. Adrian Rothschild Brown."

"Try the Home."

Bartlett turned another knob. "I think it was Gussage who said," boomed a voice, "that the point was not whether he was a bad botanist or art critic or philosopher or bridge-player or connoisseur of china, silver and furniture, but how he compared with other botanists who were also art critics, philosophers, croquet-players, connoisseurs of china, pewter and furniture. 'I can't help feeling,' and I shall always remember his deep-throated laugh – 'that I come off rather well.' "

"It's hopeless. This is Morty's evening – I'm going to bed."

"Cressida's right as usual."

"A mention like that, on the Home as well as the Third, could sell anything up to three hundred copies, if only we could get it out before Christmas – still, late January's a good time too. We must keep up an interest."

"Certainly Ginger, we must pull strings."

"Throw out feelers."

"A *balloon d'essai*."

"Ears to the ground."

"Advance publicity."

"I can see a first printing of ten or fifteen thousand."

"With that title, considering the sad circumstances."

We all went upstairs and Cressida took me up the second flight and showed me into the room which Julian Frere had last occupied. Bartlett was now across the corridor and my old room was empty. "Whereupon I will show you a chamber with a bed," she exclaimed as she threw open the door. I must have looked surprised. "Don't worry. It's only Shakespeare. My uncle Pandarus to be precise." She laughed again, the strange deep guffaw that seemed to come out as if she had been slapped suddenly on the back and was so unlike her high sibilant 'repertory' voice. "I hope you'll be comfortable. If there's anything you want, you know where to find me." She spoke quite naturally and turned to go, taking the rather long strides of a little woman who does not wish to appear so, her satin dress crackling as she walked, her trim behind rounding itself under the black material with each step, like a shiny round rock appearing and disappearing with the flux of the wave.

I examined my room, which had more privacy than the other but was barer and bleaker, with hardly any books and a small electric fire. Frere seemed to have been reading various books on the pre-Socratics and snake-worship, a selection from Riccardo and another from Kant. Then I noticed an excessively slim volume, an ancient edition of *Oxford Poetry*. I began to turn the pages – Wilfred Rowland Childe, Thomas Earp, Evan Morgan, Desmond Fitzgerald, Iris Tree, "Tom-noddy's Sons" E. H. C. Rivel (Merton), "Passacaglia for a Menelaeum", "Hyssop and Hydromel", "Malaguena for a Moorish Tea-room", "Wolfenbuttel". The "Malaguena" was quite amusing and for a moment the warmth of a youthful unhyphenated Curry Rivel appeared sandwiched in between the solider shapes of Sitwell and Huxley. I flicked on: N. Tarrant, Worcester "Glebois", "Evening", "The Bride of Ballyfaherty", Erratum. "The Bridge of Ballyfaherty". "Jim Rafferty that Quiet Man", "Saint Enogast: Sunset". "The Fourth Fool's Song from Devorguila". There was even "Oxford, a poem" by Jane Sotheran (non-collegiate):

> *"When days are long and sunny*
> *The flower of youth is blown:*
> *We waste our parent's money*
> *And Time, that is our own.*
>
> *The days grow short and colder*
> *Beyond the summer's prime,*
> *And we, ere time is older*
> *Are old before our time."*

There was a printed card to mark the passage, addressed to M. L. Gussage, Balliol.

"The next meeting of the Gassendi Society will take place Dec. 1st at the Spread Eagle Hotel, Thame, when Mr. E. H. C. Rivel (Merton) will read a paper: 'Gastrology, yes, Gastronomy, no?' A conveyence will leave the Secretary's rooms at seven p.m.

G. de L. Bartlett. Hon. Sec.

Queens."

I wondered if the whole lot had belonged: I had a feeling that I was on the brink of a discovery, but I was disconcerted to feel that Julian Frere might have made that discovery too. Otherwise the pamphlet would not have been in his room, for pencilled on the fly-leaf was "M. L. Gussage, Balliol". Then it occurred to me that I had never seen the library

which was also the room where the elders had retired to
bridge. A library should tell one everything, for although a
few books may betray many accidents, lendings, borrow-
ings, presentations, cures for insomnia and so on, a library
of any size is an infallible index of character and taste. And
who the hell was Gassendi? I thought of Oxford clubs whose
names were vaguely familiar – the Magnasco Society, the
Hyprocrites, the Railway Club, the Canning, the Clareter,
the Bullingdon, the Grid. And then I tried to sleep. After I
had put out my light and turned off the electric fire and
opened my window on to the garden I had yet to see by
daylight I lay in bed trying to imagine what this extraordinary collection of elderly people had looked like when
young. Producers and consumers – consumers disguised as
producers – what was a publisher? Does he produce or consume? I began to feel a strange uneasiness as when one wakes
up and hears the telephone ringing and with each despairing
trill has to decide whether to rush down and answer it or
whether at the moment of decision on the first step on the
stair, it is going to stop. My head buzzed and I had a sensation of intolerable tension in the solar plexus. My nerves
seemed on edge. It was like being tickled all over under an
anaesthetic with a ticklishness which was really a violent
irritation half-way to pain. I tossed and shifted and suddenly
got out of bed and put on my dressing-gown. I seemed to
have a ball of wool in the pit of my stomach which was
being wound up from some distant control tower. I opened
the door and tip-toed down the stairs, past Bartlett's door
and the landing below, down the wide bottom flight to
the hall, my breath coming quicker, my heart beating, and
slowly, silently into the sitting-room where there was still
an aroma of cigars and coffee and wood-smoke from the
dying fire. With a gathering sensation of intolerable weakness, I stumbled towards the plant-house and quietly opened

the door. The moonlight shone through the glass roof and cast a reflection of the mimosa and the tattered vine; the broad green hammock swung softly and the moon shone full on the low brow and oval face with short dark hair, snub noses and pouting lips, on the upright rounded forearm holding the rope with its mesh of short dark hairs.

"Why look who's here," laughed Cressida, "I told you you would know where to find me if you wanted anything. So what is it you want?"

"I want anything you want, Anything."

She laughed again, a low satisfied, immensely practical laugh. "Good heavens. You have climbed down. I thought we were all relegated, banished, dismissed from the class. And why do you think I want anything?" She put out one leg out of the hammock, a black silk pyjama out of which peeped a small white foot. A light rug covered her and underneath it I could see her chunky body, her legs drawn up, her hips curved like a water melon.

I saw that there was really no room except on top of her and that any sudden assault would only swing the hammock away. I felt weaker than ever. "Cressida!"

"Don't shout. I'm still here."

"Cressida, I love you. I adore you. I want you. Please. Please. Here. Now." I knelt down and steadied the swaying hammock.

She was smiling, her lips drawn back, her white teeth showing, her brown eyes seemed to hold a melting mocking expression under their long lashes.

I pulled back the rug and sank my face into her small white stomach. "Cressida."

She put her hands into my hair and I felt her hard-soft electric fingers working round my scalp and then a faint pressure pushing my head away and downwards – there was a smell of tuberoses, a knot in the pyjama cord. I moved my hand to deal with it and opened my eyes. I saw her navel like the end of a banana, the dark short hairs arrowing downward, I thought that I was going to faint. Then suddenly I seemed to feel his presence, the tall figure, the Olympian head, the magic voice. "So remember – creation is its own reward – the only pleasure and the only reward – and now I must go back to my bridge."

I stood up quickly. Lady Alice Fitzwilliam looked down from her tub, a camellia's glossy leaf brushed my cheek, *Mandevilla suaveolens* and *Semele androgyne* (a rum beggar) climbed upwards in the shadow, "and here's my first and last love, *Daphne Odora*"

"Cressida – I'm sorry. I can't. Not here. Not now – when he . . ."

"You silly boy, are you worrying about Morty? He never minded anything like that. Ours was a very adult relationship. Besides, my health requires it. Doctor Hislop told me so."

"Yes but don't you feel – I mean you were married to him. Isn't it all much harder now?"

"If you mean why aren't I crying my eyes out all day long then you know nothing about grief. You're just like all the men here, they can't bear the idea of a woman not feeling sufficiently bereaved. I know what's expected of me.

> 'Tear my bright hair and scratch my praised cheeks
> Crack my clear voice with sobs and break my heart
> With sounding Troilus . . .'

But whoever said he was Troilus?

"And now please go to bed. Nobody asked you to come down here."

"I can't go and leave you like this."

"You leave me as you found me." She had pulled back

the rug. Her face glowered up me like a spoilt monkey. It was an angry sensual childish face, but not altogether childish; there were lines showing round her neck and behind her ears. I remembered Frere's taunting her about me in that same spot and anger and lust formed a confused amalgam. I decided to beat her. "Cressida!" "Will you please go upstairs *at* once. Or must I ring, Mr. Kemble?"

"I'm terribly sorry. I don't know what possessed me to come down like this and disturb you among your memories. You must think me a cross between a rabbit and a ferret." I walked out quickly and through the sitting-room as a heart-rending "Stephen" exquisitely spoken, hardly audible, promising infinite desire and contrition followed me. Like Ulysses with the sirens, I had almost to put my fingers in my ears. My cool white bed seemed a haven of refuge. *Oxford Poetry.* No, no – *Snake Worship.* No, no, no. I plunged into the pre-Socratics which bore a printed slip on the inside cover: Tallboys library P31 . . . "The diagrams of modern stereo-chemistry have also a curiously Pythagorean appearance. We sometimes feel tempted to say that Pythagoras had really hit upon the secret of the world when he said, 'Things are numbers.' History has not been kind to the pre-Socratics . . ." I fell asleep.

Sunday morning in the country is one of the glories of life. It is a day that is apt to go bad on one but which begins with kedgeree, crime and culture as the newspapers arrive, and accelerates to the first sizzling plateful of roast beef. "No day is wholly lost," Sir Mortimer had written, "that begins by breakfast with a newspaper and ends by dinner with a friend. But Sunday I knew was ceremonious. I put on my dressing-gown and went down.

For the first time the sun was shining and I caught a glimpse of the garden, a yew hedge, carved box trees, a large tulip tree on a sloping lawn and a sprawling mulberry with leaden splints on its ancient limbs. A few yellow leaves caught the pale hard sun, the rest thickened in drifts across the shining grass to where a line of willows marked the river. Inside the dining-room a fire crackled. The sweet smell of methylated spirit exhaled from the row of silver dishes, porridge, fish-cakes, scrambled eggs and mushrooms, home-made sausages. There was a pot of smoky tea, another of hot milk and a steaming coffee machine. Bartlett and Curry Rivel were already at table. "Three to me, one to you so far," said Rivel. "Ah good morning, Kemble – perhaps you'll join us in our long-established Sunday-morning pastime."

"What is it?"

"We draw lots and each get a Sunday paper, we then score two for each mistake we find and one for each nonsensical or ridiculous statement. Then we change papers and look for mistakes the other has missed, for which we score double. The same mistake repeated in the same paper scores one. The winner is the first to score ten. If you draw a paper with book reviews of course you stand a better chance."

"I don't think our young friend is eligible," said the publisher, "he's a contributor."

"Vita Sackville West, liquidambar with an 'e' – and you missed it. Four more to me, making seven."

"Mortimer says Diderot outlived both Voltaire and Rousseau."

"So he did – two more to me for false challenge – and here's *Finnegans Wake* spelt with apostrophe s. You always miss that one, Geoffrey. It's an elementary test of observation. Well, that puts me out."

Bartlett produced the perfunctory cough which passes for laughter at that age. "Well – it's a lovely morning. You shall give me my revenge at croquet – you must play too, Kemble."

I had one sausage and the best part of the scrambled egg left, the *Sunday Recorder* propped up before me. "I'm afraid I don't know the rules."

"All the better, we have our own. You shall start on the 'Tallboys' game."

"I say, listen to this: leading article in the *Umpire* – 'And for why? Because the new Elizabethan Age has this thing in common with the old: scant use for the intellectuals. Scientists we honour – statesmen, industrialists, actors, artists, sportsmen, men of grit and vision – mark you – in every field. But not egg-heads for egg-headedness's sake. That is why the reign's first literary knighthood (late great Sir Mortimer Gussage) was not just an honour to literature but to the kind of man from whom this country wants to get its literature. The all-round, the open-air figure, the personality in its own right. Sir Mortimer was such a personality, open, steadfast, true – a great walker, a great talker, a great trencherman, a great ball-games player, a wit, a broadcaster, the kind of fellow one would pick out in a Dover customs' queue and think: "My, it's good to be back." As no doubt many times did we: Sir Walter Raleigh, Sir Henry Newbolt, Sir Arthur Quiller Couch, Sir John More, Sir Robert Boothby, Sir Beverley Baxter, Sir Ivor Brown. "Kind in hall and fierce in fray", great men, great Englishmen whose temptation when they see an egg-head is to pull a steel-shafted brassie out of the bag and address the ball.' Is this your doing, Ginger?"

"I may have dropped a few hints at the Club: many journalists are always glad of a subject and Arnold had often put in a good word for Morty at Chirnley. Isn't it splendid? Oh, if only we can get that book out before Christmas. While he's still on the boil."

It was an unfortunate expression and Curry Rivel cast a cold eye on the publisher whose thick lower lip hung out suddenly till he looked like a guilty bloodhound. "If we're going to play croquet," he faltered. "I think we should run along."

Everyone went up to dress. On my way down, I couldn't resist opening the door of Sir Mortimer's old bedroom. It seemed this morning to be completely anonymous. There were one or two books by the bed, a Vulgate, a Pléïade Montaigne and Gide's journal, a two-volume *Tom Jones* in tiny print and a *Lives of the Poets*, *The Diary of a Nobody*, Southey's *Life of Nelson*, *Eckermann's Conversations with Goethe*, Lucretius, Rabelais, Sophocles, Wordsworth, *Jarrold's Dictionary of Difficult Words* and the small *Larousse*. He seemed to have been reading Maria Edgworth's *Ennui* and there was an envelope sticking out of it. I picked it up. It was not an envelope but a printed letter from the Traveller's Club.

"Dear Morty,

I understand your difficulty. On the whole in my experience it is not usual to honour a man twice for 'services to literature' – a knighthood would not actually preclude an eventual O.M. (look at Gilbert Murray and Barrie) but Hardy, James, Mackail, Augustus were not knighted and Desmond, Walter Raleigh etc. did not get the O.M. May I suggest however that 'a bird in the hand . . .' I remember your old boast to the Gassendi Society that you would live to be a hundred but as you might have to wait another twenty for the O.M., superlative distinction though it be, I would accept what you're offered. Cressida – and all your friends and readership – would be delighted – and so would Her Majesty.

Ever yours,
Wroxeter."

I put it reverently back, touching evidence of "the last
infirmity of noble minds". There was another door beside
the bed which I had not noticed. It led into a dressing-room,
I found. I stood rooted in surprise. In one corner stood a
dozen different rackets in their presses: tennis, squash, rackets, real tennis, even badminton – in another were golf-clubs
and some fishing-rods, but what held my attention was a
row of bookshelves which ran right across the length of the
wall. They went up to eye level and were entirely filled by
some sixty pairs of boots and shoes, all with their trees, the
heels at the back, the toes pointing outwards. They were
graded into colours and shapes like an impressionist's palette
of brown and buff and mahogany-red: sometimes one pair
seemed to announce a new key and the others were so many
variations on a theme – the Norwegian slipper, the brogue,
the sandal. Riding-boots, waders, walking-shoes, evening-
shoes, black, brown, black and white, white and brown,
suede, patent leather, beige, fawn, crocodile, ostrich, red
morocco – and always like an old love to which the mind
turns back – the oft-repeated brown brogue, with London
leather, gnarled and caviare-grained, nearly always unworn
and suggesting the passage from car to train, train to boat,
cabin to boat-deck or even down a gravelled drive – of these
small fastidious active feet. A pile of canes next caught my
attention and a long closed cupboard which opened to find
another procession of greys and browns and greens and
ambers – a whole autumn woodland of jackets and suits. I
began to push them along on their hangers like beads on an
abacus. There was a Harris-tweed in brown, green and
yellow with leather on shoulders and elbows that was like a
still-life by Braque. I couldn't resist slipping into it. Too big
of course, and too long – I put my hand in each pocket and
felt one hand close on a pipe-bowl, the other on a tobacco-
pouch. There was a hint of blue from a fly in the button-

hole. And with it this plain cherrywood walking-stick, I think – and a cap. No, better still – a deer-stalker. Now for the feet. I observed myself in the long glass which lined the back of the cupboard door – the deer-stalker, though it nearly covered my face, gave me a Sherlock Holmes look, the long deep jacket and stick, the pipe in my mouth, the pouch in the other hand, not at all bad really; quite the youthful Gide, good heavens – what was in it? A golf-ball. I put it back in the pouch and frowned sternly at my own image. I saw another face behind me and whipped round.

"Mr. Kemble!" Sacharissa was still in one of her nocturnal tea-gowns. Her large purple face under its dome of hair seemed quite unsuitable.

I put back the pipe and pouch, removed the coat and hung it up, put on my own, restored the cane to its fellows and said, "I'm extremely sorry, Miss Sotheran. I'm afraid I can't possibly explain." I walked past her into the bedroom and ran as fast as I could down the stairs.

The publisher handed me a mallet. "This one should help you. It was Morty's. He was a dab at the game – in fact – he invented it." We went out on to the lawn.

"Good morning, Stephen." Cressida was wearing dark-green trousers with a little yellow jacket and a brown shirt. "I hope you slept well."

"Very well indeed, thank you."

"Ginger and I are going to take you on. We think the two 'creatives' should play together."

I noticed that though the mallets, balls and hoops were normal, the lawn was not. It sloped steeply down to the water, some of the hoops were concealed by trees, others were round corners, or behind flower-beds, it was more like a miniature golf-course.

"The rules are quite simple, the same practically as for golf-croquet; the first pair to go through a hoop wins it and we all go on to the next, no extra turns are granted, but a turn is lost if you go out, i.e. into a bed, on to a path, or in the river. We start from the mulberry and the first hoop is uphill, over there.''

The game bore the stamp of Sir Mortimer's genius, the uphill hoops required exquisite parabolas to drop back into the jaws of the hoop and the slightest tap from an opponent sent one rolling down to the stream again: the downhill hoops required even more skill and the sideways ones could be approached only from tiny mossy plateaux or by using a tree-trunk to break the trajectory.

There were screams of delight when a ball went in the river. As soon as the game began the masks seemed to fall. Curry Rivel spoke with icy irony, the publisher seemed full of angry contempt, the two tall elderly men strode about like schoolmasters refereeing their boys' football. Cressida hopped and danced crying, "Oh well done, Ginger, goody-goody." I found the game not too difficult and pleasantly ingenious. "Knock her out, a gentle tap will send her packing, *rentrez-vous Madame, à vos appartements.*" Very soon the two men were not on speaking terms and their balls sang with spite as they whizzed over the wet grass, alternately knocking each other out of position.

Cressida, however, laughed like a child. Her play was erratic and she seemed to tire easily. "Into poz now," Bartlett would chide her. "Remember position is nine-tenths of the law." It was over an hour before we managed to beat them, Bartlett hitting too hard and Cressida too wide, while Curry Rivel patiently plotted his course, approaching by invisible tufts and plantations which held the ball or sneaking drop-shots round the tree-stumps. At the end the two men strode off in silence while Cressida slipped her plump brown arm through mine as if nothing had happened. I felt weak all over. I knew that nothing could prevent me going down to

the plant-house again tonight, not even Laurian arriving.
What was happening to me?

"How do the others play," I asked her.

"Well Morty was marvellous, of course, he's done every
hoop in one – and such a sweet partner. But he cheated
sometimes. I mean he would make up new rules to make
sure of winning. Sacharissa doesn't like it. She says we fight
too much. Norman's rather good and never loses his temper,
but doesn't want to win enough, and poor dear Julian won't
take it seriously at all. He won't do anything unless he's
good at it."

"Except drink."

"It's because Hugh and Ginger are so well-matched that
they mind so much," she went on. "Each thinks he's a little
bit better than the other so they can only play with a partner
they can blame everything on." We were walking by the
river, a narrow dark stream on which the yellow willow
leaves were floating. "We must go back to the house now.
I haven't seen Sacharissa this morning."

I felt weaker than ever. Her hand lay on my arm like an
ivory paperweight. We turned towards the house and passed
a shrubbery. I dragged her aside. "What's in there?"

"Why, nothing. I go there to sunbathe. It's a kind of
maze."

I rushed at the entrance. It was indeed a maze of very
thick holly, quite impenetrable.

"Wait – shut your eyes and count a hundred," laughed
Cressida, "and then I'll give you three minutes to find me."
"And if I don't?"

"I shall put my clothes on again." She spun me round and
lightly touched my eye-lids with her little padded fingers
while I counted feverishly.

At a hundred, I turned round and flung myself at the maze
entrance. Being holly, it was impregnable and one could

neither see through it nor take any short cuts. It had to be solved like a mathematical problem. I seemed to remember some maze where you turned right and forever afterwards left. I tried that and reached a dead end. Then I began left and tried turning right. Another blank. I retreated and tried alternately left and right; it worked a little better. Suddenly I remembered the rhyme-scheme of the sonnet – a—b—b—a, a—b—b—a, c—d—c—d—c—d – left right right left, left right right left. I was crashing round the circles now with my heart thumping – how would the last rings work – right—left, right—left, right—left. I was getting closer and closer to the centre. I sprang round the last small dark circle and in through the narrow holly door. There was a little round lawn with a seat and a stone plinth in the centre, surmounted by a bronze head, the pointed beard and the ironic eye of Sir Morty. From somewhere outside I thought I heard Cressida laughing. I was furious. It was a joke in the worst possible taste. I began to run back the way I had come. But it wasn't. In my rage I had forgotten to reverse the formula which had led me to the centre. I kept running into blind endings and since I couldn't remember where I was I could not decide when to apply the formula again. I was struck by an appalling thought. I was going mad. When I tried to reason I felt a singing in my ears, an enormous vacuum behind the nose. I could die in here for all they knew or cared. I understood why rats in similar tests have nervous breakdowns. I flung myself at the holly hedge until my hands and face were bleeding. Then I tried running blindly with my eyes shut, 'Laurian, Laurian – save me.' I tripped and fell. I was flat on the grass with Sir Mortimer's bust looking down at me. I began again, I applied my formula, I walked out of the maze. When I reached the house, I fancied people looked at me curiously – a circle of ageing nobodies, ridiculous old parties when you came to look at them. Pooey.

"Have a drink," said Cressida, "or perhaps you'd like a wash first? Where *have* you been?"

"Where have *you*?" I whispered.

"Well, I gave you a very good clue. I said in three minutes I would put all my clothes on. I went and had a shower."

There was general laughter. I decided I would throw my drink in Bartlett's face.

Angelo entered the room. "Excuse me, but Mr. Kemble is wanted on the telephone from London."

I walked out with my head high. "Goodness what a lovely day – blissikins when they come in November with something one doesn't deserve," croaked Sacharissa "a secret drawer, or a cheque from the income tax."

The telephone was in the hall. I picked up the receiver. "Stephen? It's Humphrey Bowles here. Something rather disturbing has happened. I want you to come straight back."

"What, now?"

"Yes – as soon as you can. Don't stay another moment. And don't eat or drink anything. Anything mind you."

"But what shall I say?"

"Say the paper needs you."

"Three minutes." He hung up.

I rushed back to the drawing room. "Bad news, Lady Gussage – at least for me – I have to go."

"Oh dear – nothing serious, I hope."

"The paper wants me."

"What, on Sunday?"

"It's the editor – personally. He may be going to send me abroad. I must go up by the next train."

"Then you'll miss Laurian – she'll be disappointed."

"I will write to her."

"You must certainly come down again as soon as possible. We can't count this week-end."

"Yes, do," said Sacharissa, "you'll probably want another fitting."

I ignored her and turned to Bartlett, who looked genuinely concerned. "Perhaps you can tell me the next train."

"Three o'clock."

"Come along, let's have some lunch." Cressida led the way into the dining-room and Geoffrey began to carve a most succulent sirloin of beef, black on the outside, crimson within, with fresh horse-radish sauce, Yorkshire pudding and crisp roast potatoes. "I recommend with this our local ale."

"Delightful review of yours this morning," said Curry Rivel, "six novels in as many inches."

"I suppose you receive all sorts of bribes and presents?"

"I don't think so."

"I don't suggest of course that you accept them."

"And blackmail – has no struggling author or authoress tried that so far?" said Sacharissa. "We may not be criminal but we all have our foibles."

I smiled ingratiatingly. "Oh, Miss Sotheran."

"You may call me Sacharissa, boy."

"Beware of her," said Rivel, "she wears her ormolu heart on her Balenciaga sleeve."

"The manners of a Medusa."

"*Merci*, Geoffrey."

"The pleasures of a Poppaea."

"Thank you, *cher ami*."

"The grace of Our Lady of the Rocks and the wit of '*feu la demoiselle*'."

"Madame de Sevigné and Mademoiselle de Lespinasse – erudite you are!"

"And since you guessed them," beamed Curry Rivel, "erudite you too. *Brava, brava!*"

"But Mr. Kemble, you haven't eaten anything! Are you a vegetarian? Would you like something else?" Cressida seemed to express genuine concern.

"No – I'm quite all right – but I can't eat when I'm upset – train-fever, so sudden, nervous indigestion. Please don't pay any attention."

"There's nothing wrong with it, I hope?"

"No, no, it's delicious."

"Try a teeny mouthful then – here, I'll feed you – close your eyes – open your mouth."

What was I to do? Should I trust the clear mocking voice or was I going to my doom? What was that line of Leopardi about even shipwreck being sweet in such a sea? Then I remembered Laurian's words: "She would never do such a thing. She adored Daddy." I did as I was told and a delicious gobbet of red beef faintly basted with horse-radish and impaled on a crisp slice of Yorkshire pudding insinuated itself between my lips while I remained with my mouth open like a young cuckoo. "Open your eyes and shut your mouth." I found her face a few inches away from mine, her little white teeth showing, the deep laugh which was so unexpected shaking her. "And now I recommend washing it down with a noggin of ale." I took a large gulp of the clear dark faintly nutty bitter.

"How's the train-fever?" said Sacharissa. "We don't want you laid up. Shall I take your temperature?" She seemed impudently maternal – or was it not so maternal? Blackmail – we all have our foibles. I didn't like the tone. I continued to eat and took a second helping of crème brulée but I refused dessert and the inevitable glass of port with it.

"Don't pay the taxi. It's on the house," said the publisher.

"I feel already as if you're one of my young authors. I hope I shall make your fortune."

> " '*I'll make your fortune one day you'll see*
> *But first you make my fortune for me*
> *And that is why we all aver*
> *That a man's best friend is his publisher.*' "

Cressida sang the words as a calypso and it was evidently a family joke for she and Hugh and Sacharissa repeated the last two lines in harmony.

> " '*That a man's best friend is his pub – lish – er.*' "
>   girl's   her

They nearly drowned the taxi.

When I got back to London in the intolerable gloom of a November Sunday evening, I was already furious with Humphrey Bowles. He had ruined my week-end and prevented me seeing Laurian, who was expected late that evening and who alone could rescue me from my growing obsession with Cressida – and if she couldn't, there was Cressida waiting downstairs in the hammock. He had prevented that too. So I was in a very bad temper as I joined the *table d'hôte* as we liked to call it.

"Ah, thank God you're back, Kemble" (we prided ourselves on our unconventional use of surnames). "You're all right?"

"Perfectly."

"You followed my instructions?"

"Very nearly."

"What do you mean, very nearly?"

"I had a very good lunch – otherwise I've eaten nothing since breakfast."

"Good God. We'll have to have it pumped out."

"We'll do nothing of the sort." I settled down to my Italian dinner and it was not till afterwards that we were alone and could return to the subject. We went up to my room and sat in two armchairs looking out into the thin fog and sipping a brandy. "Now what is this all about?" Bowles had a thin sensitive face with a look of a typical civil servant who was also an Everest climber. He had been a bright young man in one of the secret departments at the end of the war – being just that much older than me – and I sometimes wondered how he was settling down to child psychiatry and the routine of a clinic. He had long hands with delicate spatulate fingers, a high precise voice, a slight fringe. He should have been a Rupert Brooke or Beardsley rather than a back-room boy, but he grew up at a moment when other qualities were required of him.

"You understand, of course, that I would not have signalled if I had not thought it important?"

"Yes. That's why I'm here. But you've got to prove it *was* important."

"You remember the passion fruit?"

"Yes, of course."

"I was never quite happy about it – after Van Breda identified that leaf for us – and so I've had it analysed."

"And what was in it. Arsenic?"

"No – not at all – but there were traces of something."

"Not passion, I hope."

"Tromexan, if you wish to know."

"What the hell is that?"

"Tromexan? Well it's the trade-name of the most recent of a series of commarolal derivatives, first isolated from spoiled clover hay, eating of which causes a haemorrhagic

disease in cattle. It prevents synthesis in the liver of a sub-
stance called 'prothrambin' which is essential for the clotting
of blood. Hence the blood will not clot, and were bleeding
to start while the drug is active one would bleed to death.
The drug is widely used under laboratory control and given
to out-of-hospital patients – it's naturally very useful in
phlebitis or other conditions where a clot might form with
dangerous consequences – thrombosis, for example. The
maintenance dose is about 200 milligrammes a day and
patients may be given a month's supply. If you take more
than that your blood might refuse to clot for about twelve
hours. The taste is very bitter. Now it would not be fatal to
swallow as much as this unless one were to start bleeding.
But there are some kinds of people who find it very easy to
start bleeding. There are people with a tendency to cerebral
haemorrhage of the variety known as sub-arachnoid, where
small congenital weaknesses exist in the intracerebral vessels
and normally these merely 'leak' and give rise to a severe
headache. With Tromexan an attack would be fatal. That
may be induced by trauma to the head of quite a mild
variety, and there is no way of telling if this congenital
weakness is there. There is also bleeding from the gut or
kidney to be considered, as in duodenal ulcers – and there is
often kidney bleeding in small amounts in those with high
blood-pressure. Tromexan might easily convert such an episode into a catastrophe. Cirrhosis of the liver would also be
a very dangerous condition – so would a cut shaving or even
a few scratches from a gash – like you've got."

My heart missed a beat. "Now the great Gussage I understand died from a cerebral haemorrhage, but unless the dose
of Tromexan was considerable it might not have killed him.
Tromexan put him into a condition in which a cerebral
haemorrhage was bound to be fatal and the slightest shock
might have produced such a haemorrhage. A passion fruit

would remove the bitterness of the Tromexan and it could be injected through a hypodermic syringe into a passion fruit. If it doesn't come off, no harm is done, but there is a reasonable chance that it will come off and meanwhile there's the Arokanthera, the Bushman's poison coming along – cook up the roots and get a dessert-spoonful of Onatain, a glyco-side which causes death by stoppage of the heart – ventricular fibrillation – much more deadly – but more easy to detect. Pretty fiendish. I think all things considered I was right to drag you back and I think you had better have another brandy and tell me everything you can remember about your two visits, but especially that first evening."

PART IIII

That They Might Tell Us

I have a fairly good memory and I was able to give my friend a detailed picture of everything that had happened and most of what had been said, suppressing only one or two incidents in which it could appear to one who did not know all the circumstances that I might possibly have been made to seem ridiculous. Bowles listened with immense attention.

"The crucial fact seems to me," he pronounced, "that your obituary was put in Gussage's room. It would be enough to make his blood boil because whatever we write about the dead, however favourable, is always patronising. We can never credit them with the immense complicated mechanisms of living – or with their illusions of their own greatness. Have you ever tried to count up how many people are dead? No – I don't suppose anybody ever has – rather an interesting computation, assuming the population of the world to be determinable at given times. How many living people have expired since Julius Caesar? Why do they take up so little room? And what proportion of them are known by name? And of those known by name how many has a well-educated European, Indian or Chinaman heard of? I wish one could get somebody who was serving a long prison sentence just to write down everything they knew. But everything – names, dates, places, information, filed under all the subjects. I'm not at all sure if memory, so far from containing everything we have ever learnt as it's supposed to, doesn't wipe the slate pretty clean when new facts are being continually superimposed on old ones. Memory – what is it but a fairly efficient machine for forgetting? Where was I?"

"The crucial fact, you were saying."

"Oh yes, the crucial fact is that, being famous for his rages, Sir Mortimer has only to absorb the Tromexan in his passion fruit which prevents his blood from clotting and read your obituary to send it up beyond 180, already a danger point, and the chances of one of these minute haemorrhages in the brain or the kidney are immensely increased. His blood literally boils. It's all so accidental and so all the more diabolical."

"I don't quite follow. It seems to me too accidental, too haphazard. So many things could go wrong."

"And if they should, they go wrong in such a way that no attention is called to them. There is no suspicion, the murderer has only to wait and try again."

"But supposing someone else had eaten the passion fruit?"

"They would have been in danger for a few hours, of getting cut or scratched – but only Sir Mortimer had the high blood pressure, the choleric disposition; he alone was predisposed to bleeding even as he was the most likely person to eat the fruit. I think you said his daughter had reared it as a surprise for him?"

"Yes – but it was presumably in anybody's reach while on the top of the dessert on the sideboard. She probably put it there a few hours before dinner. And anyone who knew anything about him knew that he would eat it – I mean who knew his great interest and curiosity about that kind of thing."

"Just as anyone who knew anything about Claudius knew he would eat the largest mushroom on the dish."

"Ah yes, that was talked about at dinner. The '*delectabile boletum*' someone called it."

"Who?"

"I simply can't remember."

"Well, you must try to remember. I want you to make a list of all these Latin quotations and as many of the French ones as you can recall and put the name of the speaker against each. Between them, your new friends would seem to have a pretty well stocked mind."

"What on earth for?"

"Oh it's the kind of thing we used to do in the war – helps to get a line on a person; one was looking for Nazism or Communism – find out what people read, the words they use, find out whom they see – and follow up anything incongruous, inexplicable in the picture."

"What about the police?"

"They usually took over where we left off, we gave them the gen. And in this case we have no proof so far, only a little evidence. There was no inquest, and remember – the person who knew most about the passion fruit was Sir Mortimer's daughter."

"It would be intolerable if she were subjected to interrogation."

"She won't be as long as I feel you are telling the truth to me." It was typical of Bowles that he seemed already to be sitting on the permanent side of a desk with me on the other. "One or two more points," he went on, "you are aware that you have made what we call a transference to Sir Mortimer."

"I don't know what you mean."

"Well, you have adopted him as a spiritual father – long before he adopted you – ever since your reading of *David and the Sybil* gave you the courage to shake off your own.

He can do no wrong and his daughter can't either. About his wife you are not quite so sure, for she is not his daughter's mother – and his publisher you regard with frank hostility. I wonder how much we ought to allow for this magnetic variation of the Kemble compass. For one thing you seem to have been so busy falling in love that you have failed to notice how very morbid the conversation was getting. Here is this oasis of so-called humanism, of living for beauty, art, moderation, taste, spiritual values, personal relationships, gardening and what have you – yet the talk is always about death, disease, crime or impotence. I wonder if that was by accident or design."

"It may just have been because it made them enjoy their dinner more."

"Yes, it sounds a very good dinner. A lot of money about for such a literary household."

"Why not?"

"Well, I don't wish to diminish your father fixation on Sir Mortimer but I don't think it was the profits on the Tallboys edition that enabled them to live in such style. You are a romantic, you find an oasis and climb up a palm tree, you don't speculate how the water got there."

"Any more observations?"

"None for the moment. I want you to tell me as soon as you hear from them again; I want you to agree with anything you are asked to do. I'm going to do a little research into the economic foundations of this well-run establishment. The trouble is they're all so old, nearer sixty than fifty, a lot of whisky's flowed under the bridgework by then. When you come to think of it, you and I know really absolutely nothing about these oldsters. Think how subtle, involved and malevolent must be the thought-process of an ageing biped with fifty or sixty years of cerebration behind him!"

"We know what they look like, soul speaks to soul, and we know their books, at least some of them."

"Yes, but these people are ruins by now, caricatures of their old selves, they've lost the power of action and action is what defines a man. I shall have to look up their war-records."

"That's easy enough, I expect they were all in the Ministry of Information."

"Oh, I don't mean that war – I mean their war. 1914. 'The recent unpleasantness in Flanders.' Luckily enough I have an uncle who was at Oxford about then. He might be able to tell us something."

"See if you can find out about the Gassendi Society."

"Certainly. By the way, they don't seem very keen on their contemporaries. They never quote the living, never mention the Sitwells or Forster or Valéry or Proust, let alone Auden or Sartre. It's as if a clock stopped somewhere. I wonder when it did stop and why. Thank God, I am beginning to learn a little about children at the clinic, I don't suppose writers are very different, at any rate in regard to the instinctual drives. What about aggression, for instance – where did it all go? Let's see if I can get this straight.

"Sir Mortimer was inclined to bait Mr. Norman Farran. Mr. Curry Rivel is inclined to bait Sir Mortimer. Sir Mortimer dismisses Julian Frere. Julian Frere annoys you. You take a dislike to Geoffrey Bartlett. And how about affinites – sexual urges in various states of repression – you have one for Laurian and (paternal) for Sir Mortimer, Curry Rivel is nice to Sacharissa, Cressida and Sacharissa are nice to you, the Farrans ask you to tea. You had better go next time. I'm interested in Farran, he seems the only sensible person. But equally the most suspicious."

"Why?"

"Green finger. Access to conservatory. Passion fruit

would permit familiarities from him. Makes request to Sir Mortimer after dinner which is brusquely turned down. Wants a loan I expect."

"He seemed a very mild man."

"Yes, but don't forget – they're all ruins – I wonder if he was so mild when he wrote *The Bride of Ballyfaherty*."

"Bridge not 'Bride'."

"Well we must find out."

"One more point, Bowles. We haven't got a motive."

"Oh to hell with motive – everyone has a motive for murdering everybody, ask a child. I'm looking for someone with the particular character-pattern to commit a murder."

"Still most murders – over ninety per cent, I believe – are committed for love or money."

"If you include sex maniacs under 'love'."

"I don't think there were any sex maniacs at Tallboys."

"Frere seems a bit unbalanced that way."

"Frere was the only one with a motive to get rid of me. I am convinced he took my obituary and hid it under Sir Mortimer's pillow when he was told I was to have his job."

"But what precisely was his job – apart from pleasuring your hostess?"

"And you say," I began to get excited, "you say that whoever planted the obituary must have prepared the passion fruit. In fact I don't think we have much further to look. He cooks my goose, he avenges himself on his employer and he gets Cressida."

"And a complete set of the *Dictionary of National Biography*."

"There's nothing funny in this that I can see."

"No – it's quite possible. Admittedly he would probably have to marry Cressida – and if Cressida remarries everything, I believe, goes to Miss Gussage. And he couldn't support Cressida for long on a set of the *D.N.B.*"

"Don't forget, he's been putting around the story that I'm responsible."

"Cressida – I mean Lady Gussage – might have told him about the obituary before he left. And, incidentally, it might conceivably have given him a stroke even without the Tromexan. In which case he would be perfectly right."

"It seems to me the timing is enormously important. How do you know Sir Mortimer took the Tromexan before he read my article?"

"Yes, the timing matters tremendously. I think he ate it before he went to bed because once in bed one doesn't throw skins in the waste-paper basket. And the natural place to put your obituary was under the pillow or the sheet. He may not have gone to bed for some time."

"Don't forget he had eaten half a pear and the Pitmaston pippin as well."

"In bed, presumably."

"And he had a stroke during the night and was dead about nine in the morning."

"So Miss Gussage told you."

"I think you should get one of your medical friends to work out exactly how long the necessary 200 grammes of Tromexan which prevent the blood clotting altogether require to be fully absorbed by the system. It must be some hours after taking them."

"I think so too, Kemble. You're coming along. And one wonders if possibly he did not find your obituary till the morning and one also wonders whether he had been getting Tromexan in anything else he had been eating – apples or pears or Chinese gooseberries – or even turtle soup."

"The dose might have been spread out in fact?"

"Two hundred grammes – that's about six tablets in solid form – rather a lot for one passion fruit. But it's an excellent container – skin like leather – high sugar content – and a fruit you swallow in one gulp. A brilliant idea."

"You sound very callous."

"Not as callous as some of his nearest and dearest, from your description. It doesn't sound very much like a house of mourning."

"The chief mourner wasn't there."

"Miss Gussage – yes – and Miss Sotheran sounds genuinely upset."

"I think Cressida was right when she said that none of them had realised it yet!"

"Possibly, though they had all been to the funeral. There's something very final about a country burial. It's not like a memorial service where anything might happen – transmigration, special hymn for agnostics, 'he is, we like to believe, with us in spirit' and so on. Well, we must go to bed. Try to work out who said what about the Emperor's poisoned mushroom – and sleep well. I am not convinced so far that your own life is in danger. Good night."

For a long time I lay in bed jotting down the threads of that month's old conversation, and the foreign quotations that I could remember.

"Dinner's everything – *c'est le but des actions humaines*" (Sir Mortimer). '*Les honneurs déshonorent, les titres dégradent.*' (Curry Rivel). The Roman dinner had been suggested by Frere . . . Carême on Roman cooking – *foncièrement lourde et sans finesse* (Sacharissa). Domitian's dinner described by Frere. '*Ego nolo Caesar esse*' (Sir Mortimer). "And what kind of dinner could I tempt you with Norman, a fruitarian orgy?" "Not just fruit – perhaps a few mushrooms like Claudius." "One mushroom, wasn't it," said Curry Rivel, "one very big mushroom," answered Julian, "*delectabile boletum.*" "What, you've read Suetonius too, Norman, in between chemical sprays?" "No, only Robert Graves in a

Penguin . . ." "*La table élégante est le dernier rayon de soleil qui caresse les vieillards*' (Sacharissa). '*Ut puto, concacavi me*' (Frere). '*Sempre più terribile*' (Sir Mortimer), and '*Frutta, frutta, frutta,*' '*Dov'è la ritirata*' (Cressida). '*Vino scortisque demersi*' (Sir Mortimer). '*Supportons la vie qui est peu de chose et reprisons la mort qui n'est rien du tout* (Sir Mortimer quoting Voltaire by Cressida) . . . The food-taster's request produced by Curry Rivel from Grimod de La Reynière; '*ubi sapientiae cultissima via*' (Curry Rivel) and '*il faut tenter de vivre*' 'whereupon I will show you a chamber with a bed'. But thank God, there had been no demand for the English quotations. It would have been easier to record such sayings of Cressida as were original. Finally I read myself to sleep on Sir Herbert Read. Egotism, erethism, eclecticism and escapism were the characteristic features of our own *zeitgeist* by which our literature would eventually be condemned. Not a very good outlook for Sir Mortimer. "As for escapism there is no compromise possible on this issue, to escape from life is to escape from art" and now he had escaped us all, leaving his home behind him, his family and his friends and the *aigre-douce* enigma of his prose, the Tallboys edition in its green phalanx as his only monument.

Two days of novel-reviewing sauntered by. Then Bowles invited me to his room after dinner. "Any more invitations?"

"Nothing so far."

"Well, I have been dining '*en ville*' as Sacharissa would say. I've found out quite a bit. By the way have you got the list of quotations?"

"Here you are – all complete except for '*compañeros*' and '*ma basta*' from Cressida. I can't remember when she said them."

Bowles studied my list carefully. "Let me rearrange them," he suggested. "*Citations gourmandes.*" Sir Mortimer (2): "Dinner's everything" and "*Frutta*". Curry Rivel (1):

The story from Grimod. Sacharissa (2): "Carême on Roman cooking, and the one about *'le dernier rayon'*."

"Oh, yes, the Marquis de Cussy – admired by Baudelaire – I remember now."

"Excellent."

"Frere: *'Ut puto, concacavi me.'* 'I do believe I've bogged in my bags.' Last words of Emperor Claudius. And we mustn't forget the last words of Sir Mortimer. 'Eyes look your last.' Now for the Latin. *'Delectabile boletum'*, the delicious mushroom (Julian Frere). 'Vino scortisque immersi', 'sunk in wine and sexual offences' (Sir Mortimer) and 'Where is the enormously cultured path of wisdom' (Curry Rivel). Both those quotations are from Petronius, I'm not sure they aren't from the same speech."

"Also one Voltaire to Sir Mortimer and the one about dinner I think he said came from Hoffmann."

"Fascinating – we may now express them as follows: *circa* 1805 onwards (date of Grimod de La Reynière's almanac – I've been looking him up). Sir Mortimer (1) (Hoffmann) Curry Rivel (1) Sacharissa (2). I shouldn't be surprised if that dreadful rigmarole of Lady Gussage about the bustard isn't Grimod as well. Now we come to the Roman Emperors. Frere (2) Sir Mortimer (1) (Eyes, look your last) then Petronius (contemporary of Nero) Sir M. (1) Curry Rivel (1) also (1) Voltaire, and (1) Mussolini to Sir Mortimer and Flaubert to Curry Rivel."

"And *'il faut tenter de vivre'* Valery."

"All right, Valery, if you say so – but on the whole the well-stocked mind seems particularly rich in two spots – one around the twelve Caesars (Frere, Sir Mortimer, Curry Rivel) and one around the gourmets who developed the literature of cooking which culminated in Brillat Savarin – Sir Mortimer, Curry Rivel, Lady Gussage and Miss Sotheran all come in on this. And after that very nearly a blank."

"Don't forget that it is Norman Farran who first mentions the mushrooms being poisoned and who knows most about fruit and plants."

"No, I won't forget. Here's a little more information. The Gassendi Society was a dining club run by some very dim men – aesthetes mostly – fellows who couldn't get into anything better (my uncle's information). Gussage was all right, good-looking fellow, played real tennis, splendid actor, excellent 'Mercutio', 'Horner', 'Troilus' and member of the O.U.D.S. and Grid, took a third in History. Curry Rivel, very clever, unhealthy sort of fellow, brilliant and all that kind of thing – friend of Tony Goup – created quite a stir, member of the White Rose (Jacobite Society), drew a sword-stick on a few perfectly harmless men who called round to debag him. Was sent down for flagrant immorality. Jane Sotheran, non-collegiate, handsome, dashing, ploughed in Modern Greats; Norman Farran, very dim man, played scrum half for his college, wrote poetry, quiet, a hanger-on of Gussage. Bartlett, a very bad man, hairy about the heels, always going up to London; chorus girls, night clubs, all that sort of thing. Loud suits, dirty stories. Deplorable fellow.

"War records: Gussage rejected by medical board, 'nearly broke his heart', Farran a commission in Artists' Rifles, was wounded, Curry Rivel, a conscientious objector, worked on a farm, Bartlett, something to do with embarcation and so on at Rouen. Of course they were very young when the war ended. Gussage was trying to enlist all over again as a private! Gassendi Society does not seem to have continued after they left. Gassendi, French philosopher and physicist 1592–1655. Upheld Galileo, Kepler, Hebles, Pascal and so forth. Wrote three books rehabilitating Epicurus. Opposed Descartes and founded a system of his own with eclecticism and sensualism as the base. He thought all our ideas came from our sense perceptions and attacked the mystics. Received a benefice from the Cathedral of Digne in Provence, his native city. What we should call a scientific humanist, a *'savant universal'*.

"One more story – an ancient humour to the effect that Farran was engaged to a beautiful girl with a lot of money when he went off to the war and asked Gussage to keep an eye on her. When he came back they were married. Financially his books have not done very well lately and the 'Tallboys' limited edition hasn't sold out yet. Erudition is fearfully old hat. Bartlett's firm hasn't been too prosperous either, his golden age was the late twenties and early thirties. And the war, of course, which prolonged the lives of so many publishers. It is a very overcrowded profession. I see that Curry Rivel was mixed up with the Duke of Bedford, social credit, separate peace and all that kind of thing, he was pro-France and pro-Mussolini, pro-Wittelsbach. Sir Mortimer, however, was very anti-Franco and anti-Munich, a staunch Churchillian, Lady Gussage frequented the extreme left, Bevanites and Communist peers. Miss Sotheran was all for de Gaulle and practically joined the Free French, and Norman Farran just went on fruit-farming. We nearly had to pick up Curry Rivel and put him in the 18B hive. By the way I took rather an interesting course in the war on how to foment a revolution. One was given lectures on the special kind of red rags for each bull – how to inflame various minorities, set Arabs against Jews, Romanians on Bulgarians, Serbs on Croats, Ghegs on Tosks, or start a Sicilian Vesper – interesting but I'm afraid largely theoretical. Well, next time you go down there that's what I want you to do. Develop all the latent antipathies, the stresses and tensions, until something or somebody cracks wide open. I want you to praise everybody's writing to everybody else until somebody objects, then give them all you've got. Meanwhile I hope to prepare a couple of little experiments in psychological warfare. And you might start by giving *If I were Lord*

Lundy a boost in your next review – but stick in somewhere, if you can, the words, 'It's obvious that Miss Sotheran knows nothing about the upper classes.' "

I was glad to see him go. All he had done had been to shed a load of London gossip on to me, part of the age-long accumulation of malice and envy which hangs about the literary life, a fragment of the consumer-attack on producers in which his horrible uncle seemed to have been so destructive. "We've got to find out what these people do all day, what they live on, how they did in the war" – but the whole charm of Tallboys for me was that one had no inkling of any of this. "Dinner was everything", that was the rule, and I couldn't imagine them except as I had seen them, accommodating themselves to a meal which was a feast of the mind as well as of the body as a small orchestra settles down to the music in front of it, each with his instrument to play. I had come under the spell of a conversation piece by candlelight, I had achieved the dream of every aesthete: I had walked into the picture. I didn't want it analysed. Yet I had no choice, for Bowles, if I proved recalcitrant, with his evidence, had only to go to the police and land them all with the horrors of an investigation. I was caught and if I hadn't out of vanity paraded the passion fruit and the leaf, I would not have been.

"Lady Gussage and Mr. Frere have been spotted dining in an Italian restaurant," was Bowles's next contribution. "I think you'll get your invitation now."

"I don't see the connection."

"Don't you? I expect that Bartlett is not allowed to ask you unless Lady Gussage is allowed to ask him. And by the way, why haven't you tried to get in touch with the maid of Astolat?"

"She's not in the telephone book."

"No? Her studio is in 1D Bedford Gardens. You must write."

"I don't know what to say."

"Say how sorry you were to miss her, how much your thoughts are with her at this time and perhaps suggest a very quiet meeting – tea at the Blue Cockatoo or lunch at the Esperanza."

Somehow I could not manage to; I felt guilty about Laurian, although I did not consider I had done anything blameworthy and I could not rearrange my feelings so as to write the letter. And I was furious at the news about Frere and Cressida. What right had this yahoo to force his drunken attentions on her in her great grief, her hour of mourning?

At last, three weeks after my last visit, the telephone rang. It was Geoffrey Bartlett asking me to come down on Saturday and keep my promise to go over Sir Mortimer's last manuscript. "We were all reminded of your existence by the nice things you said about *If I were Lord Lundy*: I hope you haven't forgotten ours. We publishers are only human and it does us a mint of good to know our faith in an author has been justified, that a new generation is able to perceive the beauties which have enchanted the old. The usual train then, and the taxi's on me." Nothing about my being met by Laurian. I felt considerably hurt.

Humphrey Bowles was more pleased than I. "V. sat." he exclaimed that evening. "Now for your briefing. I've got some interesting gadgets for you." He spread out a batch of magazines. "First of all I want you to mug these up. Period atmosphere." He handed me a complete set of *Wheels* and another of *Coterie* and one or two more "experimental" issues of round about 1919. "The gang's all there," he went on, "except Norman Farran, who drops out when his poems about places give way to articles about them, gardening notes in *John O'London's Weekly* and finally *Holiday Haunts in the South West* for the Southern Railway, which seems to be his swan-song. Anyhow, you needn't worry much about him. But feel your way into the rest of this and when you think you have it all straight, ask a lot of questions about the Gassendi Society. We now pass on to my two last exhibits. Here is the first. A little present to your host and hostess." He took out of its wrapping an incredibly ancient bottle, small and with a long thin neck encrusted with a heavy seal. It looked as if it had been washed up from the *Royal George* or the schooner *Hesperus*.

"What on earth is that?"

"Imperial Tokay, 1787 – and I may say I had a job getting it. I've been to nine sales for the last three days. I want you to see this gets shared out equally and I want you to record exactly what everyone says and does when they drink it. It should make you the hero of the evening and prove a great little disinhibitor."

So far he had been talking to me in his usual bantering manner, his long pointed profile hatcheted against the light, his thin fingers entwined, his green eyes aglow with the interminable private joke which he seemed to make of life, the attitude which I had noticed in young brigadiers or young men from the cabinet offices – that everybody else was rather absurd and inefficient and that everything outside their ken had to be reduced, by a series of nicknames, to the dimensions of ridicule. Suddenly he pushed his hair back, revealing a high worried forehead under the disguising fringe, and looked at me quietly. "There's only one thing I ought to say, Kemble. We think Sir Mortimer was murdered. Until we know why he was murdered we can't tell if it's necessary for anybody else to be murdered. I want you to know that you run a certain amount of risk in returning."

"Oh – as to that – don't give it the slightest thought. I can take care of myself."

"Yes – but if the murderer knows that you are investigating. And this time you will be seriously investigating."

"About the Gassendi Society?"

"No, no, you can talk your head off about that, but I want you to scour every cupboard, every bathroom to find the rest of the Tromexan, I want you to search all Tallboys and the Farrans' mill for it and to hunt around for the missing plant – people hate throwing rare plants away. I want you to comb out the bedrooms, listen at keyholes, steal letters, sow alarm and dissension everywhere – I want you to demand your obituary back before you do any work on 'Eyes, Look Your Last' and then notice who gives it you; I want you to insist on some particular section of his last book being shown to you, not just the first page they have handy. Ask to see the passage about 'those who lived at the right time' or the farewell to Archestratos, and don't be fobbed off with anything else. Make those your conditions – and above all get a good look at the one room you've never been in – the library. Find out what they do all day, every day. Open a file on the whole lot. Think yourself into those cagey old heads, those gouty anatomies – become Angelo for a bit and see if he's all he ought to be. Make love to Sacharissa."

"Then I should be in real danger."

"Yes, you are – and so I'm going to ask you whether you're prepared to do something twice as dangerous. To stick your neck out and risk losing it – to do the kind of thing some of our chaps were willing to do in the war?"

"Yes of course I am – if you tell me what I'm doing it for."

"You are doing it for truth and justice, if you like, or to keep the police out of the ladies' bedrooms, or just for the hell of it if you prefer – or even because Sir Mortimer asked you to."

"Asked me to?"

> " *'Let not the insulting foe my fame pursue*
> *But shade those laurels which descend to you.'* "

"All right. I promise."

Still with a feverish glint in his eye, the summit of Everest in sight, my friend produced another slender package. "When we used to send our chaps over to France in the war, this was one of the toys we gave them." He opened a box and took out a fountain pen. "Just take a look at it," he went on, holding it up, "quite an ordinary pen you see, with the old-fashioned Waterman method of filling by pulling out a lever at the side. Or that's what it looks like. But if you point it straight at someone and pull the lever out you'll find it is a spring trigger which releases a little invisible cannonball of one of the new nerve gases; quite enough to knock them unconscious and probably enough to kill. Our people would let one off at a German officer if they were alone in a railway compartment with him in the blackout and then pitch him out on the line. Or they could bring it out to sign a police statement and sometimes make a get-away. This one can be used only once so for God's sake mind how you handle it. Now, when you've got them all together, if possible after the Tokay's been round (don't have any yourself, by the way, you'll want an absolutely clear head), well at some late stage of the evening when they're all batting each other quotations, bring this out and tell them what it is, pass it round and keep an absolutely deadly eye on how they all react. If by any chance you should lose it then you will know you really are in danger. Don't let anyone be alone with you. Lock your door at night and see that you're always with at least one person you can trust the rest of the time. I think you can be safe with Miss Gussage, but I'm not going to recommend anybody else. If anyone points the thing at you throw a jug at them or kick it out of their hand. Still want to go through with it?"

"Certainly. I don't suppose anyone will steal it and I shall feel all the safer for having it myself."

"Good man. Keep it in its cardboard box and don't take it out even when you show it them. It's a lovely little thing: a weapon worthy of our generation. It's worse than a fer-de-lance or a Russell's viper."

"Anything more?"

"No, not for the moment. Keep your temper. Don't get provoked. Do everything you're asked. 'Keep your hands out of maid's plackets and defy the foul fiend,' and, by the bye, here's a quotation for you." He produced a scrap of paper. '*Ces gens, qui donnent de l'importance aux bons morceaux, qui songent, en s'éveillant, à ce qu'ils mangeront dans la journée, ces pretendants hommes, à les bien examiner, ne sont que des enfants de quarante ans.*' Learn it by heart and spit it out at someone. '*Cinquante ans*' would be more applicable."

"Who wrote it? One of your chaps I suppose."

"You might call him that. The name is Rousseau."

"I should like to ask you one more question, Bowles. What do *you* get out of all this?"

"Well, perhaps it's a change from cases of bed-wetting, perhaps I'm like Mallory who was asked why he wanted to climb Everest. 'Because it's there.' I dislike a mystery as much as I dislike an obstruction in the colon. And, my God, that reminds me, you must on no account let on that anything is suspected about a murder or a method, stick to flattery, alarm and dissension but don't give the show away, don't be more than a nuisance."

I had retired to bed and was deep in the *Coterie* when

there was a knock and Bowles came in again. "About your question, Kemble, what do I get out of it – what does a calculating machine get out of computing? The fulfilment of a function. I have a theory that knowledge desires to be known, that there is some kind of ratio between the facts and the brain which perceives them, the brain is greedy for them, like a sponge for water, it has a biological urge to filter information and it grows by learning. Now where puzzles and mysteries exist the brain is set a problem of analysis as well as of retention and so it goes to work on them as it would with a mathematical problem, but where the problem is too difficult or the data insufficient a kind of haunting is set up, a disease, an obsessional titivation – as a doctor has put it, 'The mind is invaded by morbid mental growths'. Now my complaint against your Tallboys crowd is that they go in for erudition, they do not tabulate and analyse their knowledge, they seem to think they acquire merit by what they know without making any use of it. Anyone can learn a list of Chinese dynasties and trot them out at dinner but there's no purpose to it. Now a discrepancy in fact – like Sir Mortimer having an empty manuscript book by his bed and Lady Gussage being able to read out of a full one – that haunts me – so does the matter of your obituary. Are you quite sure by the way that you didn't slip it under his pillow yourself just to tickle him up a bit?"

"Yes, I'm quite sure and I very much resent the question."

"Fair enough. I just felt I ought to ask you."

I went back to *Coterie*, John Rodker, S. Koteliansky, Gaudier Brzeska, Nina Hamnett.

I was delighted not to see him the next morning. My life was beginning to feel like a quiet park taken over as a battle area. Once again I took the Salisbury train, crowded and clattering, and walked the long platform to the taxi. There was no sign of Laurian, but as I patted my box of tricks on the seat beside me I began to revive. At least I was "in the picture". The final twists and turns of the valley appeared and the familiar lime avenue, now completely denuded. I tipped the driver, rang the bell; the white door opened and the peculiar smell of Tallboys, of wood-smoke and dry sherry, of calf bindings and the year's last roses disturbed me from the lighted hall. Angelo seemed pleased to welcome the *signore* and led me again to the long low drawing-room with its log fire and coloured eighteenth-century prints, its Lears and Conders, Sickerts, Tissots and Augustus Eggs, and china cupboards, the one great Bonnard of Provencal almond blossom over the chimneypiece with its French clock, the chrysanthemums in the Chinese vases, and the circle of discreet but comfortable chairs with their gilded legs and faded tapestries. The room was empty and I stopped before a strange mad painting by Dadd above a commode where a bearded river god in white china looked down the length of the room. A low stool was covered with magazines, *Country Life*, the *Field*, the journal of the Royal Horticultural Society, *Apollo*, the *Connoisseur*, the *Burlington*, the *New Yorker* – the new *N.R.F.*, and *Partisan Review*. There was a drawing of Sir Mortimer by Augustus John beside a small writing-desk, in which he looked like a pensive Mephistopheles, hesitating between thought and action, and a cartoon by Beerbhom in pale pastel colours – not a very good likeness – in which an impertinent young man with a cane surveyed a dingy group of etiolated intellectuals in short shirts and baggy trousers, "Young Mortimer Gussage, oh so definitely wondering whether it is preferable to be in Bloomsbury and not of it, or of it but not in it." I turned and Laurian was beside me. She wore a black dress and a gold Byzantine amulet hung round her neck on a black cord. Her face was longer and sadder than before; I had forgotten how completely different she was from everyone else at

Tallboys; it was not only that she had no social manner but that she was young. She did not need to be gay or pretty or anything but herself, she could afford despair – a large young body, a round fresh face, serious, composed like the expression of her enormous eyes.

"Laurian" I whispered.

She drew back, staring at me and incapable of making any conventional gesture of welcome. It was a crisis in our relationship with which I had no idea how to deal.

"I haven't attempted to see you because I have tried to understand what you have been through and the more I understood, the less I could possibly think that you would want to see me. I hoped to clear up the matter of my obituary first and even that has been impossible." My voice rang like a false coin as my confidence returned. She continued to stare at me without speaking, her eyes without expression, her lips pursed, her head slightly tilted on her strong firm back, her hands at her side.

"No," she murmured and slowly shook her head. "No."

I wanted to think she meant that it was not true, that she had wanted to see me but there was nothing equivocal about the negative, for she was looking at the ground as she spoke and seemed shaken by the force of some interior emotion. For a moment it almost seemed as if the reiterated 'no' implied a total rejection of my whole personality, which was unthinkable.

"No – not – no – my sweet – but yes, yes, yes."

She raised her eyes and seemed to look at me for the first time. The lids were pale and slightly puffy, the brown-green iris slightly transparent, the pupils large and fixed in an expression of pity and horror. She shook her head once more and her chest heaved in a despairing sob. I stepped towards her and she at once stepped back.

I heard a familiar crystal tinkle. "Ah, caught you both, *mes enfants*, spooning as we used to call it."

I joined my hands in mock supplication. "Oh, Lady Gussage!"

"Don't worry, boss, I ain't seen nothing." She skipped towards us chuckling, "Oh dear how nice it is to see you again – and Christmas getting so close – do you remember Morty's carol?" She sang a verse in throaty imitation of a village choir.

> " 'The first Nobel the angel did say
> Sir Mortimer Gussage has come a long way,
> Nobel! Nobel! Nobel! Nobel!
> Ten thousand smackers and see you in hell.' "

To my surprise, Laurian, instead of breaking down altogether as I feared, pulled herself round and even smiled. I seemed to hear at the last line an echo of a ghostly laugh – Sir Mortimer's explosive 'Ha!', which came out, I remembered, quite detached from whatever he was saying and with a faint suggestion of a bark and a menace, as if to remind one that laughter was originally a kind of abruptly curtailed aggression, the challenge of the individual to the hard.

"Sweet singing, blast pair of sirens – but continue then – *ancora*." Sacharissa now billowed like a sacred elephant, wearing a splendid dress of grey satin with mauve accoutrements and twin pagodas of some semi-precious mineral dangling from her large ears.

She was followed by Bartlett and Curry Rivel, the publisher large, leaden and florid, the "littérateur", thin, sandy and monsignorish. "That was a charming piece you wrote about Sacharissa," he greeted me; "but how could you possibly say that she knew nothing about the aristocracy – *si jeunesse savait!*" His voice rose, "You little rat."

"I'm sure I'm dying to hear him tell us what he knows himself," said Miss Sotheran. "It shouldn't take long."

"Miss Sotheran, it may interest you to know," said Geoffrey Bartlett, "could, had she chosen, have become a Marchioness."

"A mere matter of enunciation – a word of three letters instead of one of two," went on Curry Rivel, "but there's something rather vulgar about a Marquess – it's not really an English title. After all, what is a Marquess? An earl who's failed to get made a Duke, a jumped-up fellow who's only drawn attention to himself."

"That's the authentic voice of English recusancy speaking – the old Anglo-Catholic families."

"Thank you Geoffrey."

"A Rivel, a Rivel, a Reed Bool, a Dacre," bellowed Cressida.

"Dacre, Dawell, Dering, Rolles, Rivel, Saye, Sele and Thimbleby, Rivel of Curry Rivel, Rivel of Ham and Otmoor, Curry of Chew Magna and Stone – in – Oxney – an interesting skein of Saxon, Anglo-Saxon, and probably (though Burke will not go so far with me) of pre-Saxon cousinships. No titles of course were recognised by the pre-Conquest landed gentry except the semi-royal Earls or Thanes of the Heptarchy. Poverty and persecution have kept our blood pure, and pride removes us from the limelight – 'vita delicata et umbratilis' in the shadow of some ancestral manor, Hammoon or Toller, Wherne or Columbyne while the Red Rose pales before the White, Tudor usurpers yield to uncouth Stuart, Stuart to graceless German interlopers from across the heaths of Saxony. Who knows what Gods we old autochthonous families worship, which king in our hearts of hearts claims our allegiance? We have attended mass; we have ridden to evensong, the passing bells have tolled for us, but the green men, the maypole dancers and the smocked reapers who cry the wain are closer to our faith, the white Goddess, the gold wheatsheaf, the tree alphabet, the runic ogham, the Druid circles, the wisdom of Merlin are in our blood, and there are times I confess when I feel more myself among the old yews of the great Mizmaze or beside some great oak-tree in Cranbourne Chase than in Salisbury cloister or Herbert's Bemerton – or even Tallboys! William and Mary newfangledness – secular spruce and unpretentious though it be." He paused for breath and sipped his sherry. I noticed suddenly how unstoppered, as it were, he had become since Sir Mortimer's death and I remembered with horror Cressida's words – "Shove up and make room."

We went into dinner. It was a quiet meal, for there were only six of us, three men and three women, one of whom carried a lethal fountain pen in one pocket and some 1787 Tokay in the other. A leaf or two had been taken out of the table and much of the glitter had disappeared. I sat on Cressida's right, with Bartlett on her other side. Then Laurian, Curry Rivel, Sacharissa, Bartlett looked gaunt and jowly, like a bloodhound except for his military moustache; Curry Rivel a faded ginger faun, Sacharissa had the explosive violet hue of a secret drinker, Laurian was a statue of grief and yet no grief could alter the nectarine bloom of cheek and shoulder or the beautiful succulent forearm which was rolling bread in its strong fingers. This girl I knew was absolutely right for me, she had the kind of animal beauty which promises complete forgetfulness; neurosis expired on her level brow, warm lips and strong broad shoulders and yet despite all this she was not a mere winner of gymkhanas but an artist, a lover of truth and beauty, like myself. She was a well, and Cressida a flame.

"I'm afraid we're a very small party." She turned to me.

"But Julian will be here tomorrow and I expect the Farrans will be coming. In any case they want you to go to tea with them."

"We may be few – but we must enjoy ourselves," said Sacharissa. "Morty would wish it. He used to say the dead cannot come back to those who mourn them, because they can only slip sideways, into our consciousness, while it is engrossed in something else. While we are thinking of them, they cannot come in, for they like to enter by a tune, an absurd identification, a pun, a joke. Above all, a tune. Morty was so musical. The show he had chosen for his memorial service? The fandango from *The Marriage of Figaro*. He used to say he was the two notes on the flute."

"He left instructions for his memorial service?"

"No – none at all – but he used to talk about it – the Church of England burial service: he loved that – and that hymn from Prudentius – about the dead man."

"Prudentius." Rivel was off. "The first Spaniard as well as the first Christian poet, for I don't consider Martial a Spaniard, or even the Italian emperors. But Prudentius – that dry prolixity, that plutonopolis dwelling on the physical horror of martyrdom like the description of a bullfight – how Castilian! No wonder Claudel called him a great poet and tried to inflict him on the puny Gide."

"I can see you've never tried to sell Claudel," said Bartlett. "Gide's not easy, but the reviewers help and the queers lap it up – but Claudel – No sir, never again."

"I don't want Prudentius at my memorial service," cried Cressida, "I'd rather have something quite simple and unpretentious – unprudentius I was going to say."

"Like that epitaph in Golders Green on the young Jew with a carving of his racing car. 'He just blew in, and he just blew out'?"

"No, Sacharissa, something more like this:

'O that 'twere possible
After long grief and pain
To find the arms of my true love
Round me once again

A shadow flits before me,
Not thou, but like to thee:
Ah Christ that it were possible
For one short hour to see
The souls we loved, that they might tell us
What and where they be . . .' "

"You forgot the middle verse." It was Bartlett, to my surprise, who spoke and who suddenly boomed out the words, the longest speech he had ever made and which sounded all the stranger after Cressida's exquisite enunciation:

" 'When I was wont to meet her
In the silent woody places
By the home that gave me birth
We stood tranced in long embraces
Mix't with kisses sweeter sweeter
Than anything on earth.' "

"What a bad last line," said Curry Rivel, "and hardly worthy of our vicarage Baudelaire – for *Maud* and *Modern Love* and the *Fleurs du Mal* are the three last great love poems to have been written. A century without a love poem! Yeats, Hardy, Eliot may have written a few lyrics but these were all epics of love. Magic casements opening on neurosis – 'Maud' about a young fascist who goes mad, *l'enfance d'un chef* – 'Modern Love' about the ineffectual liberal bigamist. I shall have to read 'Pippa Passes.' "

"And would the team tell us," we all turned to Laurian, "since the souls we love cannot, 'what and where they do seem to be?'"

"Here in this room, round this table, in the flame, in the food." Sacharissa raised her glass, "In this wine."

"Yeats thought so, on All Soul's Eve – but I can see them as existing in the minds of their friends, who at such a gathering as this can evoke them. What do you think, Kemble?"

I looked at Curry Rivel. "The one I am thinking of exists in his books."

"Like Bergotte."

"Bergotte only existed in his books after his death. I think a great writer is smaller than his books even while he is alive. He has already put the quintessence of his life into them."

Laurian seemed to notice me for the first time. "And what about his possessions?"

We looked at the little silver candlesticks, the Laroons and the Patch and the old claret we were drinking. "No, he's absent," I cried. "These are things he has loved, but their soul is that of the craftsmen who made them. They live in them, he does not."

"Quite right," said Laurian. "But it's easy for me to answer since I'm his daughter. He lives in the way I move this arm, in everything I think and feel, in each unconscious gesture – in the heart, as Lear lived in Cordelia's; the only roof that nobody could take away."

"It would never occur to me to say he lived in one place more than another," said Cressida. "I'm still his wife – and he's just *with* me – that's all."

Bartlett leant his great face forward. "I guess he was just one hell of a damned good guy."

There was a screeching of imaginary brakes. "You've all

133

forgotten the big thing," said Curry Rivel. "Where does Joyce live? Where does every great artist preserve his unfading mortality? In his voice! Cressida – after dinner – I think we should all hear the record."

"The record?"

"Yes, Kemble – you've all heard Anna Livia, I expect. Well, Morty made a similar one a few days before his death."

"I never knew. What was it of?"

"A chapter from his new book – 'Eyes, Look Your Last'."

Laurian got up and left the table.

PART IV

Last Line

A pretty clock chimed somewhere, but time moved irregularly that evening. Sir Mortimer's voice on the imperfect record conjured with us and mesmerised us as only an actor's voice can. There was something chilly in it, a cadence I had not expected, like the first shower of winter. The cold had got into his voice and created a pool of loss and quietness around it. Then it was over, and I did not like to ask for it again. I thought it mannered, with curious echoes of his earliest style, almost like an imitation. Perhaps I was a little drunk. The mystery of the record, where the pages had been blank, might have many explanations. I found it eerie to remember it was that magical voice, an actor's voice after all, that guaranteed the style, and had somehow produced the cold words out of the air.

"Eyes look your last: lips drink your last: tell your last lies." As if the whole episode had been a spiteful illusion.

The voices of the others lapped around the edges of the silence in confident superlatives.

"What edge he had," said Ginger reverently, "even to the end."

"My dear old man," said Cressida tearfully, "the same old Morty. He had eyes of youth, he wrote verses, he spoke holiday, he smelt April and May."

Sacharissa came the nearest to criticism. "We're over-civilised," she said, "like the French generals in the eighteenth century. Have you ever read the *Encyclopédie* on the *Iliad*? I don't know who it's by."

"Not Diderot," interjected Curry Rivel. "He hated the *Iliad*."

"Maybe. This person says it's a wonderful poem even though the cooking is filthy, but now our generals have magnificent cooking and invent mayonnaise, only they never win any wars. After Morty our writers all know about cooking, only none of them can write. Except for darling Mr. Kemble, of course."

I blushed, but felt bold enough to hazard that probably it was a cook who invented mayonnaise.

Curry Rivel darted me a waspish glance. "He's certainly not over-civilised at least," he remarked. "The past does a disappearing trick, and civilisation will have to be redis-covered when all this young man stands for is over. It exists perfectly in Morty's prose, and maybe in his verse. '*Frocks up, and the nymph is over the hill.*' Better than poor Tom Eliot."

I gibbered with silent rage, but there was no reply I could offer, because I was not quite sure whether Sir Mortimer had really written it. It would be like Hugh Curry Rivel to set it as a trap.

It was Sacharissa of all people who called his bluff. "Come on Hugh, you wrote that. *Poetry from Oxford*, 1921. I still have my copy."

"I'll buy it from you if only to burn it."

"You won't. Have you lost yours? Morty was in it too, we all were. There's a copy in the library here."

"What will happen to the library now?" I asked Cressida. Although I had seen the anthology, I had never read the poem, but it suddenly seemed as interesting as the record we had just heard. Anthologies of that kind consisting of verse by the unlikeliest of poets were produced every year in those days; then as the student poets became elderly professors or journalists or politicians their verses survived to embarrass them. All these people began as poets, of course, even Norman. Probably he was still the ivy-covered ruins of one. What was it he wrote? *The Bridge of Ballyfaherty? 'Ah Balymena in the still small rain'?* They all sounded the same to me, only it dawned on me that they had something in common with Curry Rivel in one way, and very early Sir Mortimer Gussage in another: they were all three pastiche, Morty of Norman Douglas in prose and early Eliot in poetry, Curry Rivel of Aldous Huxley in both, and Norman of the Celtic Twilight, which an old aunt of mine actually remembered. She said it was a fashion in Dublin drawing-rooms when people sat about in the dark playing folk music on the harp. As for Sacharissa, she sounded like the early verse of Dorothy Sayers.

> *The sea-wind soughing and the old ships dreaming*
> *and the bright fish streaming to the twilit strand,*
> *Ah Ballyfaherty with the white waves gleaming,*
> *Ah, Ballyfaherty with the broad wet sand!*

Old fashioned, no doubt, in 1921, but not bad for an undergraduate at Worcester College; it was so poverty-stricken as an institution that only the rich could afford to live there. I knew somebody at Worcester who took four years over a pass degree in forestry. Norman Farran would have fitted in nicely. I wondered if Mortimer Gussage had once been in love with him.

"The library has to be sold alas. Have you ever seen it?"

"No, I'd love to."

"You can read Hugh's poem," added Sacharissa belligerently. "Skirts up."

"Frocks up," Curry Rivel corrected her. "Skirts up is one of Norman's flowers."

It was Cressida's turn to blush. "I prefer his fruit," she said. "What's skirt's up?"

"The common fritillary, the snake's head, the Hanging Bells of Sodom, a flower defeated by drainage because it only thrives where rivers flood. I'm surprised you can grow it here."

"Under the apple trees, that's a wet old bit of ground. I've always thought of it as the origin of the love scene in *The Sweat of the Rose*."

The Sweat of the Rose was Sir Mortimer's first novel: it had a scene of unsuccessful love-making in a damp orchard among lush flowers, an impotent attempt that gave one rheumatism just to think of. Scenes like that were new to literature in his day, but *The Sweat of the Rose* was a promising novel; it had the luck to be condemned by the Dean of Durham, an accident which made his name known, if not famous, ten years before *David and the Sibyl* burst upon the world. Still, I could see a difficulty about the wet end of Norman's orchard.

"Had he moved to Tallboys when he wrote *The Sweat of the Rose*?"

"Of course not, but he knew it, and Norman had his fruit farm. He inherited that, and as a student Morty used to stay with him. It was fruit-farming put paid to Norman's poetry if it wasn't Morty being so much better. Norman was just

138

a Georgian, and Hugh, you were just an aesthete really: Morty showed us up.

> " 'Ne voit plus fort que lui chez-soi . . .
> . . . n'oit plus sonner la diane
> D'une trompette ou d'un tambour,
> Mais plutôt au braire d'un âne,
> Au chant d'un coq ou d'une cane,
> S'éveille dès le point du jour.' "

"Good enough for you, Mr Kemble? It's a dream among Norman's wet fritillaries. It's by Nicolas Rapin, lawyer, civil servant, Provost of the merchants of Poitier, thinking how he'd like to live, just like any Georgian poet, only in Shakespeare's lifetime. Good enough for you?"

"It wasn't good enough for Daddy," said Laurian, "and I don't believe he was the kind of writer who ever stopped other people from writing, he didn't show people up. There are some artists who are so good they make you want to stop, and others just as good who simply open windows and make you want to go on."

I could have cheered this but Curry Rivel was disgruntled. "Painters may want more pictures, though let's hope not bigger ones. But all good writers want fewer books."

"Julian had it right really," added Sacharissa, pink with port. "No one had such feeling for all the things we touch and see. No one was so much for the visible world, that's what he sent you back to, not the idea of fewer books."

"Well," said Cressida firmly, "I want fewer books in this house, and if Mr Kemble wants to see the library he'd better look at it now. Laurian dear, do show him."

The library was a north-facing room like half a round tower or like the letter U, tacked on to the side of the house

about the beginning of the last century, somewhere between
Trafalgar and Waterloo, lit by three tall Gothic windows
from high up. Beyond it lay the maze and the croquet
ground, the scenes of lust and massacre. This room was the
nearest Sir Mortimer ever got to living in a castle, though
there was nothing gloomy about it. The room was bathed
and draped in light. The upper storey had an elaborate, cast-
iron gallery, and the ceiling was high above that again, with
some pretty white plaster that looked like frozen cream.
What you could see of the walls were a deep Pompeiian red
that no one can quite imitate now, not even the national
Trust, and the bookcases at floor level were three triple ones
like Gothic windows, moulded to the curve of the walls.
Even after the rest of his style of life it was an impressively
perfect room. There were not too many books for my taste,
but it was scarcely surprising that Cressida had always envied
it. It had always been Sir Mortimer's intimate refuge, as the
conservatory had been hers, so now it was going to be a
morning-room. The books, to paraphrase Auden, looked
worth every penny they were now about to fetch.

It was the modern ones that interested me, but it was easy
to make out an assortment of Voltaire. The ones up the
spiral staircase in the iron gallery were solid-looking, the
whole of Buffon for instance, a nineteenth-century Claren-
don, and an early *Encyclopédie*, and some massive bird and
flower books, but nothing really thrilling, no Audubon for
instance: just what you could have bought in 1936 or 1946
for not much money, provided you had somewhere to put
them. Almost none of them as beautifully bound, though I
did spot a seven-volume Fielding in plum-coloured calf that
the sun had faded to rose, a remarkable two-volume Tennyson of 1842, bound by Cobden-Sanderson and signed C.S.,
and an early Donne poems bound in vellum, which the fly-
leaf said was bought for just a hundred pounds in 1935.

They were the books that made their authors famous. The
Tennyson was really an early selected poems, imitating a
two-volume Wordsworth that did the same when Tennyson
was hardly born, *Lyrical Ballads* having only sold about three
hundred copies. There was not much Wordsworth in this
library except a very ordinary *Collected Poems*, which looked
worn-out and second-hand. No Georgian poets, I was
relieved to see, and the few volumes of *Poetry from Oxford*
looked rather unread. But he had a splendid collection of
Norman Douglas, including the rarest private-press editions,
and Eliot seemed to be complete down to the last pamphlet.
As a collection his library was oddly strong on poetry, which
is curious for a prose writer, as on the whole there was rather
little modern prose. He seemed to prefer exotic writers like
Apuleius and Richard of St Victor, Grimod de La Reynière's
Almanac and Brillat-Savarin, which he had in Arthur Mach-
en's translation for the Nonesuch Press. It was all a welcome
change from the standards of the *Sunday Recorder*.

Sir Mortimer's bequest to Julian of the *Dictionary of
National Biography* had already gone, leaving a long, dusty
gap among the reference books. I grubbed among the lower
shelves like a terrier, while Laurian sat in an armchair with
her long legs crossed, invigilating. She was doing a cross-
word. On the table beside her there stood a few piles of
contemporary books and new acquisitions: I remember the
works of Farquhar, so he was still interested in the theatre.
But they were an odd jumble. Someone had sent him a
typescript, asking for an opinion, I suppose, of something
called *Cucumbers and Pantaloons*, which on closer inspection
turned out to be *Uncumber and Pantaloon: some words with
stories*, with drawings on coloured paper by John Ward R.A.
I have never heard of it since; it sounded like a pseudony-
mous work of Curry Rivel, some secret sequel to *Muscat and*

Mountain. On Sir Mortimer's writing-desk lay paper as empty as heaven, but nothing new.

"What happened to his manuscripts?" I asked.

"There's nothing here except signatures in the books and a few underlinings. He had a mania about destroying manuscripts. They went to Mona Farran to be typed, then he burnt them. No one else ever saw them. He liked you to think they were dictated by an angel, like the Koran, or rather, redictated, revised, re-revised, proof-read and so on, all in the deadliest secrecy. No one else was allowed to look at them until they were perfect. Maybe he hated all his corrections."

She recrossed her wonderful legs and sucked her pencil.

"Is there a typed copy of the recording?"

"Ginger wants to issue it now as an *amuse-gueule*, but we haven't truly decided. Hugh and Ginger are literary executors, but Cressida and I own the recording, so we'd have to agree. What did you really think of it? Do you want to correct it?"

"If I could, I suppose: it's certainly tempting."

"Let's go through and find the others, then, and see if Cressida has the typescript. Do you know what time it is?"

She had sat patiently waiting for me in that library for longer than I had imagined. We went back to the living-room to find the fire just smouldering in its ashes like a cigar, and all the chairs empty and the main lights out. We flung ourselves into a deep sofa and gave ourselves a whisky and soda. The room was cold now, but it still smelt of wood-smoke with undertones of flowers and a faint erotic wave of Laurian's special smell. What was it? Half French perfume, something very light like Carven's Ma Griffe, quite different from Cressida's Arpège or Sacharissa's saxophone blast of tuberose, let alone Hugh Curry Rivel's sandalwood (Norman just smelt mildly of Pear's soap). The other half was youth and warmth, and I must admit I felt or imagined a touch of that musky animal smell which is part of the intimate attraction of women.

I found I was unable to touch my whisky. I stammered, and spoke without knowing what to say. "Laurian, I . . ."

She looked at me coolly and got up and shut the door. "No one about," she said.

"You drive me to distraction. I can't stop thinking about you."

"I don't think that's what a girl needs. We could start where we left off?"

I made a lunge. Her clothes began to slip and slide to the ground as she co-operated. We had begun to entangle, I was puffing with incredulity, when there came a crack of broken glass, and a wetness all down my left side. It was the Tokay. She saw the horror in my eyes, and felt the sticky yellow mess with disbelief. As I got up the glass tinkled, and a queer smell arose. My suit was ruined and I had brought no other. The sofa was not going to recover easily either. I was desolate, she was angry, and one could hardly blame her. I blamed myself, of course. "It's a bottle," I said, "I forgot about it."

"A bottle?"

"It was a present for all of you, but first I felt shy about it and then I forgot it. I'm so, so sorry. Whatever shall we do about the sofa?"

"It's an unusual interruption."

"I can't now. It's really put me off."

"Unusual excuse, too."

"Oh God.' I covered my face in my hands and simply wept like a child. I had taken on a duel with Tallboys out of a certain callow arrogance, and lost, this was the *coup de grâce*. She comforted me, I will say that, but when I recovered there was still the clearing up to do.

"It's a very queer bottle."

"Eighteenth-century Tokay."

"It smells rather chemical. Not magical at all."

In one of those moments of intuition that admit of no doubt at all, I realised that Bowles had tampered with the contents. He would have bought the empty bottle from a junk shop, and what it contained would be ordinary pre-war Tokay heavily laced with some kind of modern truth drug, vintage 1945 no doubt, which he was probably hoarding. I despaired of explaining, and I felt extremely sorry for myself.

Laurian sighed, "You are a booby," and left me furiously wiping among the ruins. After all, disaster had caught me teetering on the edge of the most important moment in my life so far, yet, as the philosopher says, importance isn't important but truth is. You sometimes hear of people falling in love with whole families and not individuals, yet I would have sworn I loved Laurian personally and exclusively. She was the true centre of the Tallboys maze, Cressida was only magnetic north. I felt such passion it was roaring in my ears, and at the same time all my sensations were suddenly keener. I was like a highly tuned racehorse under starter's orders. I cleaned up as best I could, got rid of the remains in the library waste-paper basket, and decided on the only therapy I knew, which was work. Laurian might yet be won, but not tonight. I fired the ridiculous fountain pen out of the window and flung the remnant after it into a shrubbery.

Sir Mortimer's working-table invited me, with its circle of yellow lamplight. It occurred to me to check the contents of his drawers. The top one had letter paper and a timetable and some catalogues for the sale of modern literary manuscripts. So the writer who destroyed his own manuscripts kept a beady eye on the price of other people's. Among a litter of paper clips, a magnifying-glass, a cigar cutter, two or three paper-knives, some typewriter eraser (aha!) and the keys of clocks, nestled what I hoped to find there, because my father had the same trick: the keys to all the other drawers. Alas, their contents were sadly uninteresting. One contained out-of-date secrets that must once have been guilty: addresses and old hotel bills and book matches, even a few ancient photographs of pretty girls, who doubtless "broke his heart by looking out of date". Only in the bottom drawer of all, the last I looked at, a big, leather-bound book of hand-made paper with deckle edges and a ribbon lay on its own. The cover was embossed with a geometrical pattern and a crest I had never seen. The whole volume was preposterously elegant, the paper faintly green, the provenance apparently Italian. More than half of it had been filled with handwriting in more than one hand. Its first page was headed with a flourish, *ACTA: The Proceedings of the Gassendi Club*. Julian Frere had been on the same trail, but I had got ahead of him at last.

I put my coat on again; the stain was clearly irreparable but perhaps I could do something with soap and water upstairs. I relocked everything, slipped *The Proceedings* under the dry part of my shirt and headed upstairs like a ghost. No one caught me or disturbed me, though I caught a sound from the conservatory which presumably was Cressida. How much had she heard of my *débâcle* with Laurian? Probably everything, but I was too tired to care, and I had *The Proceedings* to work my way through before dawn. No further adventure was going to distract me from that. I must have gone to sleep about half past three, but by then I had understood the secret of the house and of those people. I was reeling from it. When I woke late in the morning, I thought it must have been a dream, but I felt for the big manuscript book with the embossed leather cover deep under the bed, and there it still was.

I went down for breakfast in case there should still be any, bleary-eyed and, I hoped, innocent-looking, to find Hugh Curry Rivel and Ginger Bartlett still at their endless fencing match, and Sacharissa smoking. She appeared to have a hangover. Cressida and Laurian had come and gone. The tea was past its early freshness, but there was coffee, which I needed, and I found some sausages. I had formed a plan of action, of which the essential part was to pretend I still knew nothing about the past. For one thing, it would be amusing to see how much they were going to tell me. But first I must explain the proceedings of the Gassendi Club.

They used to meet once a week for discussion in college rooms, with occasional outings for grand dinners to Mr Fothergill's establishment at Thame, the Rose Revived or the Bear at Woodstock, where they were sarcastic about the food. Connoisseurship as a way of life had already started. They meticulously noted down the wine with its vintages, and they drank on a broad and ambitious scale even for those days. Fruit was noted, fish had an importance, not a cigar or a hand-made cigarette was served without being scrutinised, but over the port of the 1880s, still quite easily available then as Saintsbury witnesses, they waxed lyrical. Gevrey-Chambertin from Queen Victoria's reign was their washpot and over the obscurer Manzanillas they cast their shoe. They were a little pretentious, even a touch *farouche* in the manner of young men feeling their feet, but nothing out of the way for Oxford, a city in which every generation produces a student with a green carnation believing himself to be the first to wear one since Oscar Wilde, and every ten years sees a revival of Machiavelli's *Mandragora* in the theatre. *The Duchess of Malfi* is revived more often, and sure enough, the favourite poets of this gang seemed to be Rochester and Webster. The club appointed Sligger Urquhart as its Public Enemy, Maurice Bowra as its Advocate for the Indefensible, and Father Martindale as Advocate for the Prosecution, though not one of these elders ever attended a meeting. The members made scornful references to the Hypocrites Club. All this is necessary as background.

Their discussions of art and literature took a distinctly cynical tone, or at least when Mortimer Gussage was secretary, which was quite often. The secretary for the evening was elected on the spot after last week's read the minutes. No one could serve twice in succession, but Gussage of Balliol was one of the more frequent. And they were not only cynical, they were curiously high-minded by modern standards – cynical one may conjecture due to the post-war atmosphere, but still high-minded by culture and education. There were no other ideals at that date to which a young man could pretend. So they aspired to a serious, even to some extent a scholarly knowledge of the most decadent and the obscurest ancient literature, and to what followed that in every period. Abelard and the Archpoet, Gassendi and Giordano Bruno, Rochester and Robert Burton, and less daringly Montaigne and Voltaire. They heard a paper on Eugubinus on devils and *daimones*, and another which provoked Gussage to dry mirth about "the abysmal deeps of Personality", on Arthur Hallam's *Theodicaea Novissima*. It could all be made to sound super-respectable if not precisely academic, unless you considered that Curry Rivel was seriously interested in raising the devil, just as Eugubinus was, and in Arthur Hallam's theories of the divine in human beings Jane Sotheran had scented homosexuality.

It was important that a member who had left the University could continue to attend the Gassendi Club. After Hugh Curry Rivel's scandal and his consequent ejection from Merton and subsequently the University, they held a momentous meeting. Their project began as a joke, to help Hugh write his unwritable book, but it at once became a sort of mutual help society, including a few members now dead, one who tumbled into a deep pool of drink in some rain-nibbled, sheep-rubbed house in Ireland, and another who became a superior diplomat and a peer of the realm: both names were known to me from people's memoirs, but both had forgotten their old connection with the Gassendi Club, in one case conveniently, in the other no doubt genuinely. The surviving members entered into a conspiracy to make the book as perfect as possible and then to make it a success. Jane would write a profile of him for *Isis*, Ginger would run a feature in the *Cherwell*. Norman would print a private edition of a hundred numbered copies, and Morty would see to it they fell into the right hands: Gosse's and Arnold Bennett's, Osbert Sitwell's and Forbes Robertson's and Lord Curzon's and Asquith's. The London press was Jane Sotheran's job, because she had a cousin who was a literary editor.

But the inspirer, the organiser, the person who made it all happen, was Lucretia Dunning of Lady Margaret Hall, Norman's early girl-friend and Mortimer Gussage's first wife, Laurian's mother. Hers was the charm, hers were the high spirits, she was the link. Sad, stolid Norman had the money in those days, as he still had. Hints on the green and deckle-edged pages suggested dealings of his in modern art in France that explained how they had all lived ever since. Lucretia had died in 1935, and it occurred to me that Norman had married Mona just before the Second World War. Lucretia had animated the Gassendi Club, married Mortimer and carried him, comforted Norman and carried him, got round Curry Rivel and carried him.

The society became more and more excited by its innocent little game, but success went almost beyond its dreams and in doing so dealt it a new hand of cards. It must have become obvious to them all that what began as an Oxford sport could be played in deadly earnest in that world which lies beyond Didcot, where no one cares twopence about your degree, only about your success. The plan was not very nice, though I giggled over *The Proceedings*; the people were not nice at all. But Ginger, who spoke of the composite author being purred over by dowagers, did make it as a publisher; Hugh Curry Rivel, who thought their masterpiece really was "*comme un vin vieux qui rajeunit le sens*", became a formidable critic and connoisseur; Sacharissa was an industrious and useful reviewer, a kind of Virginia Woolf with more *oomph*, less formidable but more popular in those days. The key to their activity was a cold-blooded appreciation of the movement of taste, with a battle-plan under the vigorous direction of a small committee, who chose the writer and then revised him, or knocked together a text and then chose its reviser: both methods were suggested.

Before the Gassendi Club came to an end, it was sensibly decided that Mortimer Gussage would be better at carrying off the authorship than Hugh Curry Rivel. Hugh needed only money, he believed he could make his own reputation with his own writings, as he did in the end with *Muscat and Mountain*. Anyway it looked as if Lucretia Dunning favoured Mortimer, and Norman, who held the purse-strings more obviously in those days than he did now, assuredly favoured Lucretia. The precise division of the spoils was not in *The Proceedings*, but everyone expected to do well, and so they did. The book that appeared was *The Sweat of the Rose*. It emerged from the brief record of revisions and discussions that Lucretia Dunning, the Mrs Gussage who died in 1935, wrote a good deal of it, including the scene of unsuccessful love-making in the wet, idyllic orchard. It also appeared that by then they had every intention of going on with the game for ever.

I thought over the Tallboys Edition. Leaving aside the

criticism and art criticism, which sounded now like Lucretia and maybe Norman, and the biographies, which seemed to carry a touch of Curry Rivel, a neo-classic image in marble with the ghost of a petrified sneer, the ten great novels did yield to analysis in terms of the Gassendi Club. Sir Mortimer was such a brilliant choice: a perfect example of the last generation of humanists, the final flowering of the distant renaissance, "to which the whole creation moves". He was just what Andrew Lang had intended to be, before the failure of his epic poem, *Helen of Troy*. He had learned his accomplishments as an actor learns them, by accurate observation, memory and control. In fact he virtually was renaissance man, only hollow at the centre: the Master of I Tatti only a great modern writer, Logan Pearsall Smith only more robust, Aldous Huxley only a severer stylist, Norman Douglas without his personal tragedy or his proneness to smut. Sir Mortimer's one perfect creation was Laurian. I wondered whether she guessed at the truth of his career. It was among the pre-war generation of intellectuals he must have looked for models of the Great Man, before the newspapers had any influence: Sir Arthur Evans, for instance, or Berenson, or Belloc still unspoiled by poverty. What an extraordinary performance his had been, a work of the actor's art which was life itself.

The novels still stood, though one could spot the dominant influences, particularly Julian's in *Red and Yellow*, and *The Left Side of Venus*. He was a new recruit, an all-important dash of new blood. How the critics had praised a new astringency, an open and conscious cleverness, that seemed to come directly from France and from theoreticians no one in England had read yet. They had indeed come from Paris, but by way of Cambridge; the dancing don had conjured them up. Of course nothing gets stale so quickly as the newest fashion, so Julian was finished. I was alarmed to think what my own contribution was supposed to be: I hoped it was the revival of an old style. *Blue and Green* might be by Norman, it dealt with wartime England with almost more than the appropriate doggedness and nostalgia. Before that came *A Shilling in the Gas*, which appeared to show the influence of Orwell. I could not imagine who of them all had really written it, unless it was Lucretia's last fling; Sacharissa was much too sentimental.

It will be seen that I was working on the hypothesis of one principal writer or principal reviser for each book; if the truth were more complicated than that, or if there were other characters I knew nothing about, other Julians for example, or other women, then the entanglement was now irretrievable. The titles and the erudition of some of them were enigmatic: *Merlin in Winter* was from Tennyson masquerading as Geoffrey of Monmouth, *A Modern Extasy* suggested by its spelling a quotation from *Macbeth*, *The Sweat of the Rose* revealed by its epigraph an origin in John Donne, "Such are the sweat-drops of my mistress's breast", and *The Pleasure of Truth*, which used to be a banality but is nowadays a paradox, comes from Doctor Johnson's *Life of Milton*. *David and the Sibyl* is the most enigmatic title of all, and the best, and the greatest book. It stirs the mind to its roots. If its author was really not Sir Mortimer, then I was baffled.

As I sat down to breakfast I wondered how much of the truth they were going to spill.

"What do you feel about Morty's heroines?" I asked shambling Ginger.

"Not only in the head, are they Hugh?" he pleaded for help.

"Do you mind them?" asked Curry Rivel. "Are you prig enough to think them obscene?"

"No," I stammered. "I just wonder if they sell the books."

"An egg without a moustache is like a kiss without salt, old Dali used to say," Ginger guffawed. "They're an element, you know, an element."

"They've always been a bit ahead of their time, haven't they?"

"Ah," said Ginger wisely, "Julian said on the radio that the time may have come when to be ahead of our time we'll have to be behind the times. Where is the advance guard of an army in retreat? I thought it rather good."

"Sir Mortimer's heroines aren't an army in retreat." Curry Rivel was ready to settle me with a shovelful of Apuleius. "Then began I to deem evil of the generation of women, when I saw the Maiden was now delighted with the talk of a wicked brothel house, and other things dishonest. In this sort the consent and manners of women depended on the judgement of an Ass."

By this time I had drunk my coffee and was ready for the day. It lay before me unwasted, green underfoot and blue overhead, by some unlikely miracle of weather. I plunged my dagger into the heart of the enquiry. "Just what kind of corrections do you want me to make to the typescript?"

They glanced at each other, not at me, and Ginger played with the mustard pot. I have a curiosity about mustard pots at breakfast, ever since reading that George V used to use his to hide the turds of his pet parrot, who would insist on performing on the breakfast table, under his master's eye. The Gussage mustard pot was irreproachable and there was nothing underneath it, alas.

"The fact is, old boy, this job is confidential. You get no acknowledgement, only a good fat fee. The typescript is a bit of a muddle, fallen into the hands of secretaries and editors and so on. It's the right stuff of course, but it needs pulling together. More towards the style of *David and the Sibyl*."

"Or even *The Sweat of the Rose*," remarked Curry Rivel.

"It's hastily written and unrevised, and it needs more erudition."

"Up to a point," replied Ginger anxiously. "What it really needs is a touch more of his true original style. You're the expert on that, which is why he wanted you. He was going to ask you anyway, but then he suddenly died. Will you do it?"

"Shade those laurels that to you descend," added Curry Rivel, "*Avec plus d'art encore, et plus de barbarie.*"

"Boileau?" I hazarded.

"Voltaire," came the answer, "on the fiendish use of gunpowder in the *Henriade*, but Morty and I always thought it relevant to modern literature. We used to quote it at one another." He sighed.

I swallowed my knowledge and agreed. I was enormously flattered of course, and full of that literary hunger which is nine-tenths curiosity and only one-tenth the wish to extend one's powers. "*Plus de barbarie*" was interesting: Curry Rivel evidently thought that what the others had botched up was too bland; Ginger thought it patchy and longed for the good old days of Lucretia Gussage in her best form, rather as he might long for the great days of cricket in the 1920s, or for the great actor-managers doing Shakespeare. Was his a sense of quality, even of literature, or just a sense of performance, a sense of the past, when he was a boy in short trousers sucking a stem of grass, and all the cricketers were giants? A lot of people are passionate about good or what they call great writing, who remain inarticulate about how it differs from writers writing today. Geoffrey Bartlett can hardly have been quite the Philistine I thought he was; after all, he had had a hand in inventing Mortimer Gussage, and in deliberately modulating his perfect style.

I dressed for the day, discarding my ruined suit and hoping I could get away with a shirt and pullover and an old pair of gardening-trousers, which I had with me in case of muddy expeditions. I hid *The Proceedings of the Gassendi Club* deep in my luggage because it was too dangerous to return them to their lurking place by daylight. When somebody remembered their existence and went to remove them I would not be the first or only suspect. I rather hated to steal so beautiful a book, and so thrilling a piece of evidence for a literary historian, but for the present I was committed to continuing the fraud. If necessary, I could plead that my revision had been innocent. Ginger had produced the typescript, but not given it to me. I was to work on it in the house for a few weeks, with the surviving members of the Gassendi Club breathing down my neck, and Julian Frere available for consultation at weekends.

That left the murder still to solve. I thought I could understand why Sir Mortimer's manuscript volume of "Eyes, Look Your Last" was empty when he died, and yet now it was a fat wad of typescript. They had found the chance of one last hand at poker, the posthumous great book, simply irresistible, and possibly easier to play with Sir Mortimer absent. No one knew I had peeped at the empty pages of the notebook. What light did the nefarious doings of the Gassendi Club cast on Sir Mortimer's last night on earth? They could all blackmail each other, they were all in it together as far as I could see, with the exceptions of Laurian presumably, and Cressida maybe. So I thought blackmail had nothing to do with it. The motive had not been financial gain, nor had it been swift, immediate anger, because the crime was premeditated. The case against Norman and his mousey wife was falling flat on its face. Someone must have silenced Sir Mortimer Gussage quite cold-bloodedly because he was dangerous to one or all of them. And yet he was not

indiscreet, and he showed no tendency to repeat or to confess. The fact that he probably died of vanity and rage from
reading my obituary of him after drinking the drugged passion fruit perhaps gave particular satisfaction to someone.
Who most resented his vanity and rage I could not say. Me
perhaps.

After the *débâcle* with the Tokay, I was determined to have
nothing more to do with my seedy ex-intelligence friend or
with his friend the mysterious analyst of poisonous plants.
They knew too much already, but after the shock of the
Gassendi Club I was not in a judgemental frame of mind: I
had no intention of twining a noose for anyone. I felt Sir
Mortimer would not have wanted that, he would just like
me to get on with the job of revising and perfecting "his"
last work by his own towering standards. I would go back
to London and get leave from my paper, clear up my room,
pack another case, and say a long goodbye to the Italian
cooking. I was going to enjoy my work in this house, and
enjoy life there too; I hoped to enjoy the stormy seas of
Cressida and the deceiving deep waters of Laurian. Writing
a masterpiece, solving a mystery, and winning my first real
woman offered challenges I was ready for.

"Ah, here you are," said Cressida, "come for a tease under
the trees." She drew me out into the crisp, pale sunshine.
"Ginger says you've accepted, so I hope this is the first of
many."

"Will it be a terrible bore, having me to stay?"

"Oh no, it's lonely here, and you're fresh company."

"You must miss him a lot."

"Mm."

I felt I had intruded into a forbidden area. We walked on
in silence for a while. She swished with a bit of stick at a
large thistle like a candelabrum.

"Do you mind my messing about with his book?"

"Oh Lord no. There was always a lot of that. It was Julian for years, now it's you."

Then she was innocent of the old arrangement.

"There is a difference of course, with this very last book. If Morty had lived, I think he would have written it entirely on his own, if they'd let him."

"Why shouldn't he? Who could stop him?"

"There were furious rows about it. You know how it always is with a great artist of any kind. People surround him and live off him. They all have their roles and they keep him to themselves. They own him in the end, because they can't do what he can do, but somehow they can through him."

"You sound bitter about it."

"Wouldn't you be?"

"I feel as if I were interviewing you, under these trees."

"But I'm interviewing you, darling," she smiled seductively.

Something responded, like a bird flying up out of a bush, as they say.

"It's as if you were the only real link."

"As if. Did you know there's a philosophy called '*Als ob*'? It says nothing's true and nothing's honourable, but you have to go on living *as if*."

"You are the person closest to him – you and Laurian."

"Ah, I see a choice there, from your point of view."

"Hardly, not when I'm with you." She seemed to be emitting great waves of enchantment; I floundered in the surf. We came out into a lane where unseasonal violets nestled abundantly in a bank.

"Laurian's hard to catch. She seems friendly, she likes to act friendliness, but it's all an illusion."

"Really?"

"Something broken in her ever since her mother died. She was still very young then."

"Yes, but she's curable. She needs the Black Box like one of those overbred racehorses."

"The Black Box?"

"But you must know that. It's magic and it works from a distance. People are mad on it. They use it to cure race-horses' legs, Ginger will tell you all about it. Ginger used to have a racehorse, a great, bony, ugly brute. It bit Morty, so he hated it. Ginger tried to cure it with a black box. *La boîte noire de la bête noire*, Hugh Curry Rivel called it. I think I'll pick some of these violets."

"Can I help?"

"Oh no, if you do the magic doesn't work."

She took about a dozen with a few leaves, and we walked on, chatting away amiably enough, until we came to a wooden gate and I realised where she had brought me. It was the churchyard, grazed by a pair of enormous ewes.

"I thought you'd better see the grave," she said.

He lay beneath a small mound of scattered earth still await-ing his stone. I hate to be manoeuvred into showing feelings, but I was at least as moved as she intended, particularly when she dropped her small bunch of violets. When she gave me a solid kiss I never even gasped, just wept a bit and clung on to her.

"That's better," she said. "I wonder if the church is open?"

It was not, so she had me on a table-topped grave of the Waterloo period, hidden among discreet trees behind the vestry, in a stony wilderness of skulls and scythes and rustic angels. Of course I was bewildered, thrilled, delighted and dazed, all at once. It seemed clear to me that it was her I loved and that what was sprouting between me and Laurian, from whom I suspected she had deliberately stolen me, was childish by comparison. I did not think she had murdered her husband, but if she had I would have been on her side. The visit to the grave had sealed the matter. Yet her manner continued astringent, she was curing me of something fast and for ever, if it was only youth. I was dragged, all but carried through a gate, from literature and the love of it into life and living, where I would have to fend for myself, but I might, I just might become a real writer. This surprising experience was Sir Mortimer Gussage's impertinent bequest to me: he had foreseen the end of my education.

As we emerged into the pre-lunch daylight of the lane, she demurely quoted Voltaire on *Amitié:* ' "*C'est un contrat tacite entre deux personnes sensibles et vertueuses*'. He says *sensibles* because he doesn't mean monks, and *vertueuses* because '*les méchants n'ont que des complices, les voluptueux ont des compagnons de débauche, les princes ont des courtesans, les hommes vertueux ont seuls des amis*'. I may have forgotten some of it but those are the important parts. Oh, '*les hommes oisifs ont des liaisons*', I think that's true, don't you?"

"I should like to be an *ami*, but I'm not sure if I'm virtuous enough."

"Are you loyal?"

"Mm, to the moment, I suppose to any and every moment. At least that's my ideal."

"Good, you must tell me all the moments."

"That would take a long time."

"Well, we have a lot of talking to do, if we're really going to be *amis*."

We found the others waiting for us. It seemed to me that they knew. Laurian glowered and hid behind her cigarette smoke. She talked to the latest arrival, Julian. The others shot us sardonic glances. I was determined to brave things out, beginning with a direct attack.

"Returned to the fold," said Julian obscurely, of himself or of me?

"I wonder if I could have back my obituary of Sir Mortimer Gussage? I hope you found it instructive."

"Expendable in a way, aren't they? And yours was expended."

"It was not published. Someone stole it from me in this house."

"Don't blame poor Julian," said Cressida. "He just spotted it, I snitched it. We were consumed with curiosity."

"Who has it now?"

"Morty had it last. He was thrilled with it."

"But the doctor said – "

"Yes, it was very convenient. I mean it *could* have killed him, if he'd been someone else."

"Then who has it now? Have you, Julian?" I asked, feebly forcing my attack to its last gasp.

"Not I, I don't even remember it very well. Lacked magic, as Handsome Johnny would have said."

"Handsome Johnny?"

"Johnny Lehmann, dear boy. Maybe the doctor has stored it up against you as evidence."

Against this blank wall I battered my head. I decided to recoil and try another line of ground later on.

"As a writer, and as Julian's successor, you still have to win your spurs," said Curry Rivel, not as unkindly as usual, "but be worthy of this champagne." He handed me a glass paler than straw, with the faintest sparkles. "Salon blanc de blancs, from Le Mesnil-sur-Oger, from that last vintage of the war that the Germans never got their hands on, the last year in history when it looked as if nothing could go wrong."

"There's a treat," said Sacharissa. "The year we stopped digging for victory. What a relief that was."

"A toast to Morty in his grave, whose cellar it comes from," put in Cressida. "The old fantastical Duke of Dark Corners."

"Thunder shall not so awake the beds of eels," remarked Julian with a sarcastic expression.

"What are we eating?" asked Laurian.

"A private festival," said Cressida. "*Pâté de foie frais*, and then lobsters that were caught on Friday, from Cornwall, to match our silver salad bowl – don't be frightened, it has a glass lining for the squeamish, and last of all a honey soufflé, so we'd better be on time. Bring your glasses in."

The feast was as delicious as it promised, consisting almost entirely of first courses. It ended with apples, and an ancient Pomerol, almost faded, as soft and generous as spring rain. It must all have been devised a week in advance. The lobsters were split down the middle, and the wine-spattered butler brought it with bowls of warm water and pieces of lemon for our fingers, and batteries of silver instruments like shell-crackers and those long claw-extractors which I always find a severe test of skill. At least they muted the conversation a little. I found myself between Cressida, after whom I fear I probably languished cow-eyed, and Ginger, a cheerful and formidable eater.

"All the food of the Round Table," he beamed. "If you suppose the *pâté* comes from the French coast, the lobsters from Tintagel, and the honey from Camelot."

"Nothing from Caerleon-on-Usk."

"Oh yes," he added. "There's a bit of goat's cheese we're specially fond of, served hot as a savoury. She forgot that. The goats live near Caerleon."

"And a little dish of Roman figs," added Hugh. "Norman ripens them, but his are over."

"Nothing from Amesbury," grumbled Julian.

"Oh, yes," said Sacharissa. "Morty had a secret wine

merchant in Amesbury, who could get this champagne. He was in France in the cavalry at the end of the war."

"Why Amesbury?" I played into their hands.

"Guinevere retired to Amesbury according to Malory," Julian informed me, 'and Lancelot was in the cavalry. I always wondered why Amesbury. It was a day's journey from the grave of Arthur. I imagine that was at Stonehenge. Glastonbury's too far."

"Ah, *les pierres pendues*," added Curry Rivel, "the French for the Hanging Stones. Malory might have thought Arthur was buried there."

"Or at Silbury Hill," mooned Sacharissa.

"The whole of Salisbury Plain is studded with tumps and tombs and tumuli," remarked the practical Ginger. "Could be anywhere."

"There used to be bustards on Salisbury Plain," added Cressida, "but I suppose the foxes got them. Morty belonged to a society for reintroducing them."

"I shouldn't think a fox could get a great bustard," I said, "they're enormous."

"You'd be surprised," she replied demurely, "what birds a vixen can get if she puts her mind to it."

I was too much abashed by this to venture any more remarks about the Round Table, so I tried to turn the conversation. "How long have you been a publisher, Mr Bartlett?" I asked innocently.

"Twenty-two," he answered. "Nineteen twenty-two. After I got out of the army, which I did quite early because I was in remounts, you know, and that folded up completely in 1918. I did a few months with old Jock Murray, Byron's publisher, Byron's relics, Byron's ghost very nearly, then I went up to Oxford and whoosh, back into publishing. Of course those were easier days. If you came from a decent regiment, which has never quite been the same thing as a decent war record, and if you had a degree from a reasonable college, you just walked in you know. Sherry with the directors and welcome my dear boy. They'd been starved of young men for four years, and of course it was still a gentleman's profession when I started. Books by amateurs, meant to be read by amateurs, published by amateurs, sold an automatic two or three thousand copies and you made a profit."

"I see. And you printed Mortimer Gussage from the beginning?"

"Nearly the beginning, yes. You might say I was in on it from the beginning. But he was the new wave, cut through the others like a knife through butter. Quality you know, and always being one move ahead of the field."

"I quite see."

"Mind you, it doesn't do to be too far ahead of the field. That might be your trouble I'd say, something to watch anyway."

"What's your formula for success?"

"Oh the unexpected taste you know, the goat's cheese in the smooth salad. The hated cypress, the only tree that follows its brief master: the death shadow in an Arcadian landscape. That always sells."

"Death?"

"Yes, what we subconsciously expect, what we're secretly hungry for. Death, the cypress tree. Lawrence was on to that, but of course he got it all mixed up with sex, and most of us aren't really hungry for that, but death always sells."

I wondered.

"Funny thing, you know, this isn't the kind of conversation you could ever have with Morty. He had his own ideas, too fluent for me."

"But his sales turned out quite well?"

"Up and down, up and down. When an author's established every book sells better than the last, but not over thirty years. Times change and so do writers. Look at Belloc, he was finished in 1914, yet he went on turning out book after book. He only died the other day. The trouble was that everything he wrote could have been written in 1910. Look at Wells and Bennett and Bernard Shaw. It's the same story. But then look at Evelyn Waugh, look at George Orwell. They may not improve but they certainly alter. And Eliot alters more than anyone. Perhaps it's a gift of our generation."

"There are literary periods when nothing alters," put in Julian. "For instance, the *Causeries de Lundi* to the death of Henry James. But there are other periods like the middle of this century when social change imposes literary change."

"Baudelaire loved and envied Ste-Beuve," said Curry Rivel, "for never having had to admire anything but the beautiful."

"Bau loved the Beau," put in Julian spitefully, "he was bound to for Freudian reasons."

"The opposite." Sacharissa rallied to the support of her friend. "Bau was most ambivalent about the Beau, he invented a new beau. What he said was that he envied Ste-Beuve for never having to worship any other god. Between Baudelaire and *le beau* comes Ste-Beuve."

"And between Flaubert and his flow the *roman fleuve*." They were at it again as they had been my first evening. Once again I had to retire from the conversation. They began to argue about people who could see their own eye through a mirror while it was being operated on, but Sacharissa capped them with the Victorian Lord Harris, whose great-grandfather was wounded at Bunker's Hill and then trepanned, and arranged to see the inside of his own brain through a series of mirrors all around the room. From this they moved to a Roman emperor who was so frightened of assassination that he lived alone in a room lined and floored and topped with mirrors,

"Just like Horace's bedroom built for sex," Curry Rivel added. "Attended by one faithful servant, but the servant was corrupted and murdered him, so that he saw his own death by stabbing in infinite receding avenues of mirrors."

This was my opportunity. "Do you think Sir Mortimer was murdered? And if he was, did he know it?" I put the questions to Sacharissa.

"Those are two unpalatable questions," she answered.

"But yes, I think in some subtle way he was murdered, and I think he expected it, he even chose it, because his writing wasn't going as well as he pretended, he was getting to be like a hollow shell. So I expect he knew, though not as clearly as the Roman emperor."

"More like a hermit crab," I hazarded, "a real animal peering out of a hollow shell it chooses to live in."

She gave me a sharp look and said, "Yes, there was something of that about him."

" *'Je te salue, heureuse et profitable mort,*
  Des extrèmes douleurs médecin et confort'," quoted Ginger unexpectedly.

" *'Consolatrice affreusement laurée,'* " added Julian venomously. There was a silence broken by laughter, as if the mourning period was over. It was like the end of the Two Minutes' silence on Armistice Day, when people break out into uneasy conversation.

"Morty a crab," laughed Cressida a little too boisterously.

" 'Here you have seen a mighty king his child I wish to incest bring'. Not you, Laurian."

"Indeed not me."

"And he, good Prince, having all lost
  By waves from coast to coast is tost."

"More like a hermit crab than a human being. But aren't

you quoting *Pericles* again? Isn't that about two different people?"

"Still it's full of morals," said Sacharissa.

"And full of quotations, like *Hamlet*," boomed Ginger, taking a long pull at his Pomerol.

I had already got out of Sacharissa what I most wanted, an implied admission of how much they all knew, and how much more they supposed. The emperor dying in mirrors was itself a dissolving image of his death. It was a climax, there was nothing sudden about it to anyone but me. In fact I felt like someone who comes into the cinema for the end of the film, when the last few minutes make it look like a murder story, but then he stays to see the film round, and discovers quite a different work of art, of which death is only the end. I remembered inconsequently that films have eight reels, and the car chase is always supposed to occur in the seventh. I did not see any necessity for a car chase. It was arranged that after my tea with Norman I was to go back to London for a night before returning to work on "Eyes, Look Your Last". I expected to find it a muddle, but at least the bones, or if not the bones at least the flesh of a book. I felt like one of those sculptors' assistants who physically made most of the busts of the neo-classic period. I felt almost like the man who was called in to shave off the excessive whiskers of Thackeray's bust in Westminster Abbey, in the presence of the Dean and of Thackeray's family.

The long lunch slid smoothly towards its close. Maybe this was our car chase, only we were on a luxury train journey instead of in sports cars; I remember feeling then there was little left that I failed to understand. I know I realised how everyone around this table had been equally in the dark, all fumbling, each of them capable of murder, yet each of them loving the victim and sorrowing for him. The story had taken up so much of their lives. Anyway that was how I saw things as coffee was served.

"A great reputation," Ginger beamed over his cigar, "is like an airship. Tied to a mast, then away it floats, without any power you can see, but a thing of beauty on its own."

"Is that what you felt about Sir Mortimer?"

"Among us he was like dear old Noël Coward, do you know him? His mother kept a lodging-house in Ebury Street and we were a bit like that you know: all different, but friends, all living in rooms. Noël had a room at the top, at the back. Then as he got a bit richer he took over the top floor, and then it was the first floor, the *piano nobile*, until in the end he had the whole house. We started in Yeoman's Row, in a little house where you'd put a White Russian mistress in, then it was Bryanston Square: more room, you know, it wasn't snobbery, snobbery went rather the other way. Norman was always down here of course. Then he bought this, and Morty rented it."

"Didn't he own it?"

"Oh Lord no, only a long-term tenancy. That goes on, even though he's dead. We all pay our bit."

"Then who stood to profit by his death?"

"Profit, Laurian, maybe, Cressida to some extent, no one really. We all stood to lose: pay more and earn less."

All this was news to me, and I must admit it flung me back into my old confusion. "Did everyone earn by his books?"

"That's it. We were all tied together by contract years ago."

"Does that date from the Gassendi Club?"

"That's it; what do you know about that?"

"Only what I've heard here."

"It was a mutual help organisation that started out as an

Oxford club. We shall tie you in, if you pass muster with 'Eyes, Look Your Last'."

"I suppose I should have a contract."

"Of course. I'll have the usual one drawn up for you this week. You get a percentage on anything you revise, and a few thousand in advance. With a print run of 30,000 copies to start with, you could have six thousand advance, and say five per cent. For any further printings you get more."

It was beyond my dreams. In those days six thousand was a large income, and I was going to get it for six weeks' work at the most.

"What do you mean by anything I revise? There isn't any more after this book?"

"Oh provided it remains absolutely confidential, there's no telling what we may find among his papers. Lost early works, film scripts. There's no reason it shouldn't go on for ever. See us out anyway. And you'll be free to write other books of your own, which I'm sure I'll be pleased to publish. If you keep to your side of the bargain, there's no reason why you shouldn't be the new Sir Mortimer Gussage, hand-made for your own generation."

The audacity of the scheme was awe-inspiring. Small wonder that Julian was furious to be sacked. But his money would still be coming in for at least three best-selling novels. Sir Mortimer's death was not going to profit him. He was out of the game only as Sacharissa was. She seemed to be content enough; I thought she must have been in love with the great man. I wondered why she was called Sacharissa: a sugary, silly enough name as Doctor Johnson pointed out in the *Life of Waller*. I must ask about it. I could foresee Curry Rivel being strong on the subject of sugar: slave labour and the corruption of English taste with cheap sugar, which had surely come in with tea and coffee, reaching its height in Johnson's day but scarcely known in Waller's. To Waller

Sacharissa was still an exotic name. Or was it from some obscure early opera, French no doubt, that Mortimer Gussage knew and Samuel Johnson missed? I must ask.

I muttered something modest and deprecating to Ginger and turned back to Cressida. "What time do you think Norman and Mona are expecting me?"

"Why now. We never finish lunch till tea-time. You have a quarter of a mile to walk off lunch. They'll expect you to walk round all the hothouses and orchards before tea. Afterwards it gets dark and there'll be a mist tonight, ground-mist by tea-time and who knows what later. Anyway, you have your train to catch."

"I thought I could take my bag and leave from there."

"Good, I'll tell the taxi. Laurian, will you walk him down?"

"Of course." She swung her long legs like getting off a horse. I still admired her eyes. Yet my contract was with her stepmother, signed but not witnessed among the tombstones where Sir Mortimer lay enigmatically at rest. The prospect of a walk alone with Laurian was both exciting and alarming, but not much could happen, I thought, on a quarter of an hour's stroll across country on a late-autumn evening with the ground-mist swirling round our knees.

"Well, goodbye then, Lady Gussage. I'll be down here by the train that arrives for dinner tomorrow, if that's all right. And thank you for everything. Thank you everybody."

"It's for us to thank you, Mr. Kemble."

"Oh – "

"Go along now or you'll be late. We can have our talk in the conservatory tomorrow night."

Those hanging curtains of leaf and trailing branches of mysterious fruits and flowers were still for me a Shakespearean unknown, an unexplored, barely experienced island of delights. All the same I thought I might take just a brother and sister kiss from Laurian.

"I hope we're friends," I said, as the circling jackdaws cawed in the last of the light.

"Friends?"

" *'C'est un contrat tacite entre deux personnes sensibles et vertueuses'.*"

"Not on those terms. I'm not *sensible* and you're not *vertueux.*"

"I want us to be friends."

"I don't know what it is you really want down here, but you're certainly having a thorough snuffle round my family. Cressida gave you her lewdest and most possessive smile."

"I wasn't hunting, I was hunted. I was set up."

"When was it?"

"Before lunch."

"You aren't a very restrained man, are you? No proper feelings, only curiosity."

"Not now; I'm beginning to accept your father's death, there are no more mysteries."

"Don't be too sure of that. I liked you better when your only motive was appeasing his ghost."

She formed her lips into a kiss she chose not to give or to receive. Suddenly she was gone. A dog was barking.

The farmhouse loomed above me with lamp-light yellow in its windows, bulky among stricken-looking orchards. Near the front door a vast, arthritic pear-tree stood alone, contorted with pain. The secret of Norman's inherited wealth had been well kept, but here it revealed itself. The building itself sprawled extensively, and once you got indoors you could not fail to notice the pictures, or the fifteenth-century grandeur of the fireplace. Over it hung a large portrait of one of Picasso's mistresses, flanked on either side by two older pictures of saltimbanques with perfect bodies and unhappy eyes, which must have been painted at least thirty years earlier. Mona had been working on a type-script at a long table as old as the house. Her typewriter looked elderly too, and pleasant, homely things were strewn everywhere: a basket of fresh apples, a cardigan, the woofing dog, an untidy bunch of lavender and so on. She asked me what my writing was like. "I expect I'll be having to get used to it in future." Once again, I noticed the assumption that the old game was going on for ever, with me as Sir Mortimer. It filled me with panic now, and a certain resentment.

"You needn't worry," Norman's voice came from behind me.

"He'll step into Sir Mortimer's shoes."

"I don't think anyone could do that."

"You'll see, Mr. Kemble, you'll see."

Mona took my coat and bag. There was no servant in sight, and she wandered off to make the tea, with a placid, pleasurable glance at us both. As Cressida had said, Norman offered to take me round the greenhouse before the light failed. They had a few dim electric lights, but they were no miracle of modern science. Here and there a pane of glass was cracked, and they all smelt of ancient humus. All the same, taken together they were a remarkable display.

"You can't grow everything," he said, "so I just concentrate on what we like: the fruit and the early spring vegetables and a few flowers, and then some queer bushes I happen to be fond of."

"You seem to grow nearly everything."

"Pomona's my goddess, not Flora. The Romans hated Flora, did you know that? She made the fruit trees flower early so the frost got them. They preferred a normal season. Flora was coupled with Robigo: Flora and Robigo, Blossom and Mildew, the two enemies."

"And what's in here?" We had come to the last in a line of greenhouses, which opened at right angles to the others, behind an old wooden door and some blackened glass, as if he were ashamed of it.

"Oh, that's my temple of mysteries. They're queer plants I happen to like." He let me in with a large key.

I knew we were close to the end of the problem of Sir Mortimer's death as soon as I stepped inside. Behind a screen of dangling green and purple I could surely see the weird bush from the conservatory up at the house, and near it grew the fatal passion fruit.

I was unable to restrain an exclamation. "Isn't that deadly?"

"Only if you bleed after drinking its juice," answered Norman tranquilly.

"Suppose I told you someone had injected the passion fruit with it?"

"Gussage's passion fruit," he said. It was not a question. "How did you know that?"

"I'm afraid I had it analysed, when everyone seemed to think it was me murdered him."

"So that's where the skin of the passion fruit went. I thought it must be you that took it."

"But did you inject it, knowing he'd eat it?"

"Of course I injected it. Gussage knew. Why do you think he took it away to eat it on its own?"

"Do you mean he died by suicide?"

"Not necessarily. Look at this, isn't it a beauty? The Indian Nepenthe. And we grow aconite and hellebore, those pots over there are foxgloves. I like toxic plants, and today of course they're coming into their own. Doctors have too much power to prolong life. I cultivate the power to end it painlessly. 'Come away, come away death.' No plastic bag, no pills. People worry about how to end their lives swiftly when the time comes. I can help them. I've made up packets of seeds and so on, for everyone in the house who's ever asked for them. But that passion fruit was my masterpiece. What a pity I shall never get the credit."

"They just die? Without an inquest?"

"It's easy enough. If you use a natural method, then the death looks natural."

"It sounds ominously simple."

"It's quite legal to grow the plants. I know a man in Scotland who runs an entire garden of poisonous plants, he's famous for it, and people come to visit it like the geese at Slimbridge and the topiary at Levens. What is it Horace says?

'The god himself will loose me, when I choose.
By this I believe he intended death.
Death is the last line underneath accounts.' "

"But look here, I did overhear a row you had with Sir Mortimer on the night he died. What was that about?"

"I could argue that was none of your business. But how much did you hear? Just the end?"

"He was refusing something; he was quite angry."

"Yes, he was. We were very old friends and that quarrel goes back a long way. He took my fiancée you know, after the first war. But I don't blame him for that, I'd have taken his. We were very close. Perhaps I will tell you, but it involves other people's secrets."

"If you mean the Gassendi Club, I'm afraid I know about that too. I found *The Proceedings of the Gassendi Club.*"

"Did you indeed? My, but you have been ferreting. Then I suppose you'd better know the rest."

We went back into the house and sat down by the fire. He

hit the logs with a poker until they blazed up.

"Stephen knows almost everything about Gussage's death," he said to Mona, "so I'm going to tell him the rest." She went on tranquilly serving tea, in big cups of thin porcelain with flowers on them.

"You have to go back to those early days after the war. When we faked that first book it was going to be by Hugh Curry Rivel. But we saw that wouldn't have done. He was too preposterous in those days, and we had to alter the prose style out of all recognition. Now the obvious person to be a great writer, the obvious person to be a success, was Mortimer. Not me, I was a craftsman, nothing more, and of course not Sacharissa or Ginger. It had to be Mortimer. But Gussage couldn't write. All the rest of us have written books of our own, except poor old Ginger, and even he talks about his memoirs. But Mortimer Gussage was too impatient. When he tried it was terribly bad and came out in fragments. He was the most wonderful conversationalist, and he could act the great man: in fact as time went on, he grew into the part. He almost believed he had written all those books in the end, and so did we, almost. That was the trouble, you see."

I was stupefied with interest. I longed to ask questions, but it was better just to listen, so I said, "I see."

"He finally let us know, when you were already on the way, that he intended to write a book on his own, 'Eyes Look Your Last'. After all, we all had done, so why not him? But of course we couldn't allow it, because it wouldn't have been any good. The critics would have sneered at it, he'd have been ruined. What you heard the end of was my begging him to leave it alone and let us do it. He was adamant. And then he went up to bed. I gave him a Cape gooseberry: he loved those but he had an allergy to them, they made his mouth bleed. Did he know what that would do, combined with the passion fruit? We shall never find out, because when I last saw him he still hadn't eaten the passion fruit. He knew what was in it, mind, but I don't think he'd quite decided. It was an experiment, a kind of Russian roulette. I'd crept up there to see him, in case maybe his mood might have altered. I can tell you that he was very pleased with your article, crowing with delight over it, but I fear that might have confirmed him. After all, what a way to go out, what a really funny joke to play on the lot of us. That was Mortimer Gussage."

Mona said, "Julian knew nothing about the injection in the passion fruit. We wouldn't trust him with poisons, he was too unbalanced. It was Julian who spread those wicked rumours about you. We felt very guilty about that. Still, they died down, didn't they? And of course we didn't tell Lady Gussage quite everything either. She was so young, and she'd be so upset. We hope you'll keep the secret."

"Of course he will," said Norman. "He's the new Mortimer Gussage. Heavens, that's your taxi."

So I took my coat and bag and drove through the darkness and the smell of mist to Salisbury station. High above my head the moon melted in *beurre blanc* among vestigial points of fire. I knew I would keep the secret from Cressida and from everyone else. Moral utilitarianism left the calculus of what best to do balanced on a knife-edge, as far as I could see. Naturally I took the easiest course of action. But lying back in my empty first-class carriage to London I began to sort out my notes, and just for insurance I started to write this narrative, which now I have finished, even though I do not ever expect to publish it. No one is going to look these pages over from the privileged position of a complete outsider.